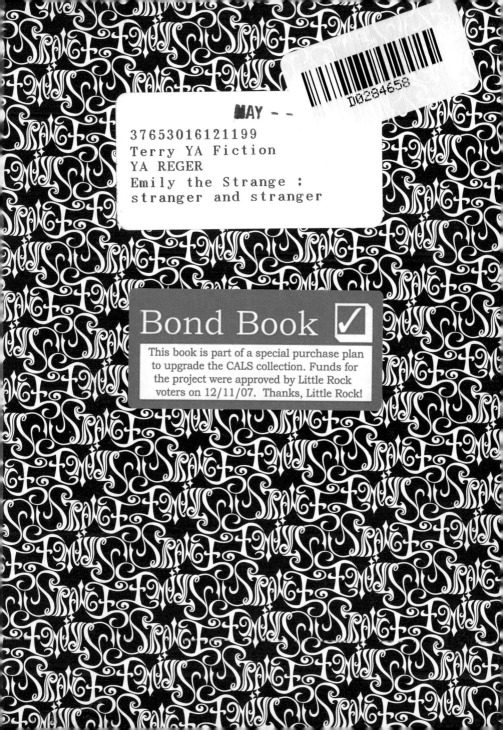

Also Strange:

Emily the Strange: The Lost Days

Stranger and Stranger

Rob Reger *and* Jessica Gruner

Emily®
the Strange
Stranger and Stranger

Illustrated by

Rob Reger *and* Buzz Parker

HARPER

An Imprint of HarperCollins Publishers

Emily the Strange: Stranger and Stranger
Copyright © 2010 Cosmic Debris Etc., Inc.

Library of Congress Cataloging-in-Publication Data
Reger, Rob.
    Emily the Strange : stranger and stranger / Rob Reger and Jessica
Gruner ; illustrated by Rob Reger and Buzz Parker. — 1st ed.
        p.   cm.
    Summary: After moving to a new town with her mother, Emily the
Strange finds her troubles multiplying when she accidentally duplicates
herself.
    ISBN 978-0-06-145232-1 (trade bdg.) — ISBN 978-0-06-145233-8 (lib. bdg.)
    [1. Goth culture (Subculture)—Fiction. 2. Individuality—Fiction.]
I. Gruner, Jessica. II. Parker, Buzz, ill. III. Title.
PZ7.R2587Ep 2010   2009007289
[Fic]—dc22   CIP
                                                                              AC

Typography by Amy Ryan
10 11 12 13   SCP   10 9 8 7 6 5 4 3 2 1
❖
First Edition

For the twins Stevee and Aimee

Self-portrait with Boxes, Cats, and Procrastination.

May 27

procrastination units, 13; new diaries started, 1; boxes packed, 0

Am starting a new diary as a way to put off packing all my stuff into boxes like Mom has been asking and asking and asking me to do for the past five days. Am not super happy about moving again. Was kind of enjoying the town of Blandindulle. Yes, it may be bland and dull, but I've finally made it my own. Had settled into a strict routine of late-night prowls around town with the cats, daredevil skateboarding, virtuo-spastic guitar sessions on the roof, crazed feral mural art, and a touch of harmless public prankery. Summer is practically here, the nights are balmy, and I am young, and I would much rather be up to unauthorized, outdoor-style mischief than sitting in my room packing boxes as instructed.

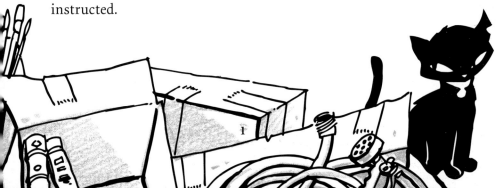

Mom—beginning her moving-out meltdown!

Later

Am back. Got interrupted by knock on bedroom door. Mom. Assured her I was packing. Am not packing. Am headed outside.

Later

Am loitering in bushes outside Zenith's Junk Shoppe and feeling terrible future-nostalgia for this place and its lovely, lovely Dumpsters, which have given me so many treasures over the past several months.

Am having trouble keeping Sabbath quiet. He has a crush on Zenith's cat, Fiona, and wants the world to know. Oh—here comes Zenith now—

Later

Am now hunkered down behind someone's garage. Zenith is torn up that we are moving. Not just because I was his best customer, but because he has a sad, unrequited crush on my golem. Had to advise him that Raven was unlikely to call him from our new town, and that he should really set his sights on a human woman instead.

We let Sabbath and Fiona enjoy some alone time while I took a last tour around the shop.

ME:	Thanks for letting me do all my shopping in the middle of the night, man.
ZENITH:	Yeah, well, what other time of day are ya gonna need a replacement control grid for a tube amp?
ME:	Or a new electrostatic ion thruster for my favorite slingshot?
Z:	Or a black-light painting of Marlene Dietrich?

Yeah, Zenith's been good to me. Will have to think of a nice going-away present for him.

Goodbye to Zenith and Fiona!

May 28

procrastination units, 23; boxes packed, 7; cats discombobulated, 4

The Packing Effort has begun, but slowly. No thanks to the cats. They know what it means when the cardboard boxes come out and are even less excited to be moving than I am. Am enduring a lot of passive-aggressive feline behavior right now. For example:

1. Violent headbutts from Sabbath are making it tough for me to write in my journal. Legibly, anyway.
2. Miles has shredded 17 cardboard boxes. Now I have to go scrounge through the supermarket Dumpsters for 17 more.
3. Any boxes left open and empty (and not shredded by Miles) have been disgustingly defiled by NeeChee.
4. Mystery has developed an uncanny talent for falling asleep on whatever it is I'm planning to pack next.
5. When not doing any of the above, all four have been milling about the room yelling "Now! Now! Now!!!!" at me.
6. Whatever it is that they want to happen "Now" is totally unclear.
7. Bowls of kibble and water have been spilled all over the floor. I refuse to say what is happening with the cat box.
8. Mom thinks I am not feeding the cats, since they are

going to her and demanding handouts of snack treats.

9. Rolls of packing tape have been chewed to sticky shreds. Have had to tie up my boxes with twine like they did in thee oldene dayes.

10. Am not enjoying peaceful four-feline blanket while I sleep. No, the felines are spending our prime nightmare hours clawing my face and biting my scalp instead.

11. Drastic increase in number of cat-puke puddles.

12. Cat-puke puddles contain more of my hair than they really should.

13. Unspeakable stench on 73% of my belongings.

Later

Am completely sick of my room, my stuff, and all those empty boxes, which do nothing but mock me. Have consulted the Magic 8 Ball for advice, and the answer was very clear:

Can't someone else do it?

Have instructed Raven to pack up all the boxes. I really don't expect much on that front. Nevertheless, am heading outside for blessed prankery and general neighborhood goodbyes.

Later

Cats and I are sprawled out on the steps of City Hall, pretending to be protesting something. We'd probably be attracting a lot of attention if it weren't the middle of the night.

Am glad that Blandindulle's population has an early bedtime. Am future-nostalgic for that aspect of this place. Am afraid we may end up in a town that prides itself on having a "thriving nightlife." BLLLLLLEAARG*%HHH!!!!!

OK, am moving on to pranktime. Am planning a little revenge on Drew and Sherry—these ridiculous lowballs down the block who like to drive around town in the middle of the night with their car absolutely full of smoke, narrowly missing feline pedestrians. Will show them what fear tastes like!!!

Later

Have just recovered from long fit of intense belly-busting laughter at Drew and Sherry's expense. It was PERFECT!!! I'd made a special batch of invisible ink that only shows up when it's exposed to smoke. Then I used it to paint sinister faces on their car windows. Then I followed them on my skateboard so I wouldn't miss any of the action. As soon as the air inside the car got foul enough, POP, the spooky faces appeared on all the windows; and then AIEEEEE, Drew and Sherry freaked out, as expected; and then CRASH, they promptly banged into a phone pole. I called in an anonymous tip to the police and bailed.

Life is good here!!!!!!!!!!!!!!!!!!!!!! I do not want to move.

Later—back in my disaster of a bedroom

Returned to find that Raven had packed all the empty boxes inside one another like Russian nesting dolls.

Man, Raven truly is the Amelia Bedelia of the golem world. Am irked at self for not giving better instructions.

Later

Have started to catalog and dismantle all the science projects in progress in my room. Here are some of the more interesting ones:

1. Prototype of English-to-Catlish translator.

2. Method of connecting my Magic 8 Ball to electronic readerboards across the nation, so that everyone can get the benefits of its amazing advice.

3. Partially completed sun-spigot, which I hope will allow me to keep plants alive in my sunproof bedroom.

4. Tests of various waste products (cat hair, lint, eyelashes, dirty-dish scrapings, dead flies . . .) and their suitability as building materials when highly compressed.

5. Jar of liquid black rock that I got from my ancestral home. Have been carefully pondering potential uses for it, as it is too precious to experiment with frivolously.

6. Superior haircolor for Mom so she can quit the haircolor-related panics she goes into every three weeks or so when the pink isn't pink enough or the blue isn't blue enough.

7. No-drip candlestick. It's made of a special metal I created myself, which is so phenomenally dense, so incredibly heavy, that no matter how you try to tilt this candlestick, it always points straight down toward the center of the earth. Goodbye, unwanted wax drips! Unfortunately, I would need a crane to lift it, and if dropped it would

probably fall straight through the floorboards and bury itself in substrata rock far beneath the earth's surface. Small details to iron out.

8. Theremin windchime.

9. Improvement on the cat-cams I'm already using. It's great to be able to review what the cats have seen and done each day, but I need cat-cams that also deliver painful shocks to anyone (besides me) who touches one of my Posse.

10. Treadmill that the cats can use to generate electricity and start earning their keep around here. The treadmill works great; I just can't figure out how to motivate cats to use it.

11. Coding that will give Raven a little more initiative. I mean, I realize she is just a golem and can only do what she's programmed for. And I appreciate how she follows my every command, I really do. The thing is, it takes FOREVER to give her all the commands she needs for even the simplest tasks. It's one thing to get her to hold a cavity resonator steady for me while I spit-shine it; but ask her to tidy up the room, and it's just blank stares and "Huhhhhhhh?" All I'm saying is, it would be nice to get a more holistic approach to the whole command

The CATS' plan for the treadmill.

thing, and I wouldn't mind if she could maybe interpret hints and suggestions. You know, I'm only one person. I could use some help around here!!

12. Laundry detergent that blackens even the whitest of clothing.

13. Duplication device. Just THINK of the mischief I can get into when this little beauty is finally functional. Ah, someday!!!!! (rubbing hands together, cackling madly)

Later

Have had a brainwave!!!!! Am going to donate all of my belongings to science and begin anew after the move. YESSSSSSS! ANEW!!!!!!!!!!! This solves the entire packing problem!!!!! Will call Science tomorrow and have them back a truck up to the house. Am feeling very brilliant.

Sun is rising; time for bed.

May 29

procrastination units, 123; boxes packed, 8; belongings donated to science, 0

Am not sure what I was thinking yesterday. Am donating NOTHING. It is ALL precious, and it ALL comes!

Later

Only three days left before we leave, and I still haven't come up with an idea for a Master Prank. It's always been a matter of personal pride for me to pull off at least one jaw-dropping prank of great magnitude in every town I live in, one that the townspeople will talk about for years. Am sorry to say that Blandindulle pranking has been more about quantity than quality.

Sigh. Am heading out to look for inspiration. Will report back later.

3 minutes later

Was intercepted by Mom at the front door and have returned to my room to continue packing. Will need to use bedroom window to escape house next time.

Must . . . continue . . . packing . . .

Later

Am back from brief (Very Brief) trip outdoors. Was intercepted by Mom under my bedroom window. She has given me a thorough shaming. It was very cute!! She has not put the effort into a real down-home shaming in a long time. Am determined to make it worth her while and pack at least one box before the night is over.

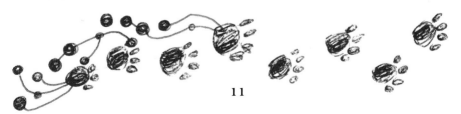

Later

Finished packing one box, then was filled with glorious sense of accomplishment, then rode that sense of accomplishment right out the basement window and into the beautiful night. Have spent a few hours tooling around town with the cats. Am now hiding out behind the hardware store watching Miles and NeeChee cooperatively stalk rodents. It is hilariously vicious, yet nonproductive, since I always intervene before things turn deadly. Best moments are when Sabbath unwittingly blows their cover, and then they cooperatively give him a beatdown. AHAHHAHAHHAHHAHAH!

Am going to miss this place. Have spent months learning where the good Dumpsters and rodent lairs are. And getting to know the neighbors' shortcomings and vulnerabilities, so I can prank them more effectively. And handcrafting wondrous pathways through all their backyards.

Oh man, I am REEEEEEALLY going to miss my wondrous handcrafted pathways!!!!! Have documented the highlights for future inspiration:

1. Specially camouflaged ladder made of tree boughs that leads over my back fence into the Gehweilers' yard.

2. Tunnel leading from the Gehweilers' yard, going completely under the Tolentinos' yard (and their DOG), and exiting in the Hernandezes' yard.

3. Seemingly random pile of oak barrels forming a lovely staircase that leads out of the Hernandezes' yard and into the Rogerses' yard.

4. Rope ladder behind the Rogerses' garage that leads to the Brookses' yard.

5. Series of small footholds cut into the Brookses' fence enabling E-Z access into the Pedersens' yard.

6. Strategic placement of dense shrubbery throughout the Pedersens' yard that provides perfect cover for anyone wishing to slip unnoticed into the Fontaines' yard.

7. Fake rock hidden under the Fontaines' deck that contains a key to their basement door.

8. Pathway through the piles of antiques in the Fontaines' basement leading to the front of the house, where only a sheet of plywood blocks the way outside.

9. Baseball hidden in long grass in the Fontaines' front yard, providing a handy excuse for anyone who might be caught exploring there.

10. Elaborate mechanism, installed inside hollow tree in the Turners' front yard and easily activated by dropping in a baseball, that opens the Turners' back gate.

11. Series of trellises and drainpipes that provide a quick way

up over the Turners' back fence and onto the Batines' roof.

12. Covert catapult (disguised as elaborate satellite dish) useful for launching oneself from the Batines' roof onto the Bacas' roof.

13. Zipline leading from the Bacas' roof back into my own yard.

Later

AMAZING. Was just walking past Drew and Sherry's house and saw them come out, so I hid, then followed on my skateboard when they drove away. Would you believe it only took them five minutes to fill their car with smoke, AGAIN? And then the spooky faces popped out at them, AGAIN; and I heard them both scream, AGAIN; then they ran the car up on the sidewalk and banged into a stop sign.

Called the police and bailed.

Have laughed so hard, I pretty much did the equivalent of a million sit-ups.

Dude. Drew and Sherry are not bright.

May 30

procrastination units, 1,123; Master Pranks dreamed up, still 0; boxes packed, still 8; admonishment units, 18

Have not packed a single thing today. Managed for a while to give Mom the illusion that I was packing by zooming all over the house, collecting my treasured belongings from various hidey-holes under floorboards, behind false panels, and inside the walls. Then had to endure a mild Mom freakout when she discovered that my tally of packed boxes had not risen at all and that, ACTUALLY, I was busy drawing up blueprints of the brilliant trapdoors and booby traps I'd built in the house over the last several months.

She was not happy.

greased rollers

secret walls
book trigger

to bedroom?

MOM: I see what you're doing, E. You're trying to bamboozle me into believing you're finally packing your stuff, when actually you're just . . . drawing it.

ME: Well . . . it may not be packing per se, but it's RELATED to packing.

M: E . . . . [deep breathing]

Managed to get her calmed down and out of my hair for the night so that I could finish up the blueprints. Am not too worried. She has freaked out like this before when we moved. I think it may be just one of those phases parents go through.

Later

Ohhhhh YESSSSSSS! Have come up with the ultimate Master Prank idea! Am going to finish my duplication device, then make a perfect duplicate of every person in Blandindulle!!! And possibly some of their pets!!!!!!! Then sit back and watch the mayhem!!!!!!!!!!!

BWWAAHAHHHAHHAHAHHAHAH!

Later

Step one of Master Prank idea is giving me some problems. Duplication device is going to be exceedingly complex to build, and I have already packed away my radiac abrasive lightning rod, capacitance-array silly straws, and multi-tined solder engine. Have built a prototype out of Popsicle sticks, but it fails to duplicate anything more solid than balled-up spiderwebs.

I guess I should feel encouraged that I managed to duplicate balled-up spiderwebs, but A) the duplicates seem more flimsy and colorless than they should be, and B) believe me, I already have more than enough spiderwebs in my life. Hate to admit defeat, but I may have to revisit this project after the move.

Later

Have been feeling very down about the move, the problematic duplicator, and the lack of magnificent Master Prank. Have spent the past few hours lying in my basement sensory deprivation chamber with Mystery sitting on my chest. I told her all my woes, and she purred at me until I felt better. Am reminding myself that new towns are fun, that I was at least able to duplicate balled-up spiderwebs, and that I inflicted many, many impressive pranks on the people of Blandindulle, so I may as well quit sulking and get on with my packing.

May 31

procrastination units, 17; boxes packed, 23; Blandindulle successes catalogued, 13

Am still kinda disappointed at having no amazing Master Prank for Blandindulle, but am reminding myself that, really, any common prankster worth her salt would drool over MY list of accomplishments. Hm, probably should not go into detail just in case this diary falls into the wrong hands. Oh glutkegs, I guess this diary's pretty much GOT to include the incriminating stuff or I'll have nothing to write about.

Later

Was interrupted by Mom just now. She threatened to withhold food until I am done packing. Just one of our little mother-daughter jokes. She knows I can easily synthesize all the foodstuffs I might need right here in my bedroom lab. Still, I can see she means business, so I assured her I would DEFINITELY get some quality packing accomplished tonight. Since it IS our last night here and all.

But first, back to the incriminating stuff, with a list of my top Blandindulle pranks. No particular order.

1. Made well-tailored clothing for all 9 public statues in town. Black dresses, to be exact. Dressed them all one moonless

13¢

BLANDINDULLE HERALD

MYSTERIOUS PLAGUE OF BLACK DRESSES DESCENDS ON TOWN

Statues of Forefathers Humiliated

night. Great photos in newspaper the next day.

2. Broadcast pirate TV show interrupting prime time for silent footage of bees.

3. Infiltrated beverage packing plant and surreptitiously inserted 2,300 plastic mice into 2,300 bottles of beverage.

4. Built telecom interrupter, misdirecting 665 phone calls to random numbers.

5. Followed Blandindulle Police Cruiser #9 on its journeys one fateful evening. And all through the night, no matter where Officers Fadler and Skint went, they smelled burnt toast. AHAAHHAAHAHHAHHAHAA!

6. Threw huge cat-only party in the cemetery. Townspeople not pleased about subsequent feline fecal desecration of the lawn. But we did it for the dead! (Note: We Did It for the Dead = brilliant name for a band!!!!)

7. Chopped hole in my basement leading to town sewers, then slogged through said sewers into public buildings, then spied on elected officials in said buildings, then rearranged the office drawers of said officials.

8. Arranged for Mom to win 50 bucks in a contest she never even entered.

9. Threw my voice a lot: 7 fully developed characters. 47 townspeople hoodwinked. Good times.

10. Got the local scientific community riled up by publishing analysis of my recent advances in singularity theory. Anonymously. While they hotly debated my identity, I short-sheeted their beds.

11. Designed, handcrafted, marketed, and sold a popular line of scarves. Unbeknownst to the purchasers, I had knitted hilarious images into them, which only the color-blind could see.

12. Built perfectly official-looking roadblocks to cut off traffic to streets where I decided cars were no longer welcome.

13. Used nail scissors to carefully snip certain inflammatory images into certain neighbors' front lawns.

Yeah, I've got a lot of fond memories of this town. And NO interest in packing.

Later

Possessions that are very hard to pack:

1. Bottles of my patented Revenge-in-a-Jar—you break one of these in a vehicle and you might as well drive it straight to the junkyard; the stuff is that stinky.
2. Crash-test dummies—the old porcelain kind, anyway.
3. Matchstick model of the bone church of Kutná Hora. (Note: Bone Church = amazing name for a band!!!!!!)
4. 88 live eels.
5. The toys of 4 cats. They are everywhere, under everything, stuck to everything, contributing nothing to the Packing Effort, distracting cats, thereby distracting me from the Packing Effort.
6. My lovely, lovely Oddisee and all its auxiliary devices.
7. Great-Aunt Millie—she's elusive like that.
8. The 5-foot-by-7-foot section of wall I did my first public mural on.
9. Pitchblende.
10. My collection of minuscule rocks. These are rocks so tiny, any normal person would see them as colorless, indistinguishable, infinitesimal grains of sand. Grains of sand, chuh!!! These rocks, which have worn down from giants over the eons? These ones, formerly boulders of immeasurable girth, history,

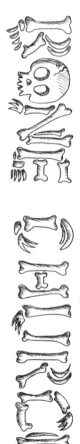

ZAP!

and footprint? How unique, masterful, and compelling each one is! Unfortunately, they're also really easy to lose if you have to pack them.

11. Collection of cat whiskers—because the temptation to hurl them into the rug like wee spears is too intense for me.

12. The annexes, passageways, ramps, dumbwaiters, and substories I've constructed on this house since we moved in.

13. Every . . . single . . . other . . . frabbing . . . thing.

Luckily I have SOME help, although I can't really take the time right now to program Raven for packing, and trying to direct her to help me has been going a little bit like this:

Me: OK, Raven, wrap this chandelier in tissue and put it in a box.

RAVEN: Uhhhh . . . K. [Walking toward my lab. Grabbing test tubes full of tissue samples. Fleshy, festering, DISEASED tissue samples.]

ME: [Envisioning my chandelier wrapped in diseased tissue samples. Yes, yes, very striking, but we have no time for avant-garde interior decorating right now.] No, Raven . . . ehhh, never mind.

SIGH. At least she's got the strength of five men and can carry all my bulky items down to the moving van for me. Hooray for my superstrong golem!!! I am not lifting anything!!!!

Much Later

Have lifted approximately 923 bulky items. With all the moving we do, you'd think I would have less stuff.

June 1
sleep units, 0; boxes packed, 1 million; new towns selected, 1

Spent the entire night and most of today packing stuff, removing miscellaneous surveillance equipment from the house, eliminating traces of my presence here, and saying goodbye to favorite spots. In the panic of the last few moments, I called Zenith and told him that, as my going-away present to him, he could help himself to anything I couldn't pack. He was over here within seven minutes with a moving van of his own. He seemed incredibly happy with whatever he managed to scrounge, though it looked like a lot of balled-up spiderwebs and broken guitar strings to me. (I think he was just as disappointed as I was that the incredibly heavy no-drip candlestick could not be lifted by any means and is staying right where it is, buried in the floorboards.)

So. Goodbye, Blandindulle.

Am now in cab of moving van with Mom and cats, headed out. Raven and Great-Aunt Millie are packed away in the back with our stuff. Mystery is curled up on my lap, asleep and purring. Man, nothing fazes her. Miles and NeeChee are obviously bothered by vehicle travel but way too cool to show it, so they are squatting on the floor, glaring at my feet. Sabbath had to be restrained and is busy trying to eat his way out of the cat carrier and/or deafen us with his yowling. Undignified!!

Later

Asked Mom where we were headed, and she handed me the map and said it was my turn to pick. Silifordville, here we come! Hey, it may not have the MOST hilarious name of any town I've lived in, but it's only 56 miles away—that's 610 miles closer than Boody, and I'm hungry. We can move to Boody next time!

Later

Have been crushed by sudden attack of anxiety over

what the new town will be like. Part of me is raring to go get lost in a new place where everything is unknown and just waiting for me to discover and exploit it. And another part of me is huddled in the fetal position, rocking and weeping, afeard that they will have no junk shops for me there.

—Oh flamjars, here's our exit, will write later—

Later

Am sitting in the cab of the moving van outside the real-estate office, sending hopeful vibes in Mom's direction. Am banking on her finding us a house with enough room for all my stuff. Attic, basement, preferably a subbasement or two, some outbuildings if possible, nice big yard ESSENTIAL, treehouse would be nice, detached laboratory not too much to hope for . . .

Here comes Mom! Fingers crossed!

MUCH Later

Have lifted all those bulky items AGAIN. GAHHHHHH!!!

At least our new house is decent—three stories, attic and basement, big yard with giant trees. No detached lab, but I'll make do. Cats have been released and are busy marking territory. Have left Great-Aunt Millie's traveling jar open in the doorway to the attic so that she can take her time getting used to the new haunting grounds. Have claimed third floor for myself. Second floor will be for whatever family antiques I don't decide to use in my room. Mom's bedroom will be on the first floor. She knows by now it's smart to keep at least one whole floor between her bedroom and my experiments.

Have also had first conversation with new neighbor.

NEIGHBOR LADY:	It's just so nice to see someone finally moving into the old Carrico place!
ME:	[Ears pricking up.] Oh yeah? Has it been empty for decades or something? Is it haunted? Cursed? Built over an Indian graveyard?
NL:	[Taken aback.] Uh, no, dear, nothing like that. It just . . . needed a new paint job, probably.
ME:	[Losing interest. Silently removing myself from conversation.]
MOM:	Well, that's good to hear. We certainly don't need any more poltergeists in our lives.
NL:	Oh my! Isn't that cute? What . . . Oh . . . AIEEEEEEEE!
M:	EMILY! GET YOUR ROBOT WEASEL BACK IN THE HOUSE RIGHT AWAY! Sorry about that, ma'am, very sorry, just an old science experiment of my daughter's, absolutely nothing to worry about, of course I'll be

happy to pay any doctor's bills, and why don't we just step across the street for a few moments...?

Welcome to the neighborhood!

Later

New task of unpacking all these boxes awaits me. It's OK, I like the unpacking half of the equation more than the packing. Will always find a couple of boxes that haven't been opened in years. No end to the treasures.

Later

Top 13 things I've unpacked that I kind of forgot I had:

1. Four cat leashes—AHAHHAHHAHAHHAHHA!...As if.
2. Spider cemetery full of precious dried-up 8-legged little carcasses that I made for a school project when I was, like, 6.
3. All-purpose emergency kit consisting of paper clip, detonator, can of spray paint, black licorice ration, cat treat ration, tube sock, and stick of gum.
4. Unfinished manuscript titled Cats of the World, in which I describe all the cats in the world. No, not every BREED of

cat. Every INDIVIDUAL cat.

5. The perpetual-motion machine, dark-energy generator, and cold-fusion cell that the military-industrial complex is paying me to forget I invented.

6. Photo of me with the antigravity machine I made for a school science fair. I'm wearing a red ribbon that says "Most Unusual Project." Chaaaaa!

7. Hilarious statuettes of past teachers of mine, made from spitballs and gum.

8. Unmailed fan letters to Dr. Frankenstein, Madeline Usher, Dorian Gray, Audrina Adare, Emily St. Aubert, and Volkert the Necromancer.

9. Customized chess set featuring hand-carved miniatures of the last 18 Junior National Slingshot Champions. The ones before me, that is.

Most Unusual Project

10. Full 66-volume set of the Encyclopedia Transylvania.

11. Souvenir hunk of shrapnel from ill-fated (but well-meaning) 4th of July celebration that involved a septic tank and some heavy explosives.

12. Shriveled monkey's paw, oozing raw evil, that I am much too smart to use.

13. Antique birdcage large enough for an ostrich or an adult-sized golem.

Later

Just woke up from long nap. Had crashed out on floorboards, totally exhausted. Will get back into my normal nocturnal schedule as soon as my room is knocked into shape.

About five minutes later

Am not knocking room into shape tonight. Am pooped. Have not been having my usual excellent nightmares. Happens every time we move. Mystery is pawing at me to say that it is snuggle time. Must get some sleep.

June 2

boxes unpacked, 1 million; rooms knocked into shape, 1; golems programmed to respond to hints and suggestions, 1

Spent a couple of hours working on Raven's programming so she can be more useful to me in the Unpacking Effort. Not easy, but well worthwhile, because my room is now completely light-proofed, furnished, and decorated, and in just one night!!! In thee bad olde dayes, it would have taken roughly 123 separate commands to get Raven to unpack a box and put away the contents. But tonight all I had to say was, "Raven, let's knock this room into shape!"

And we did.

Best touch so far is the huge antique birdcage, which I set up in one corner of the room. Then suggested to Raven that she would look really cool inside it. She got right in and sat on the perch. True, you have to know she has the brain of a raven to

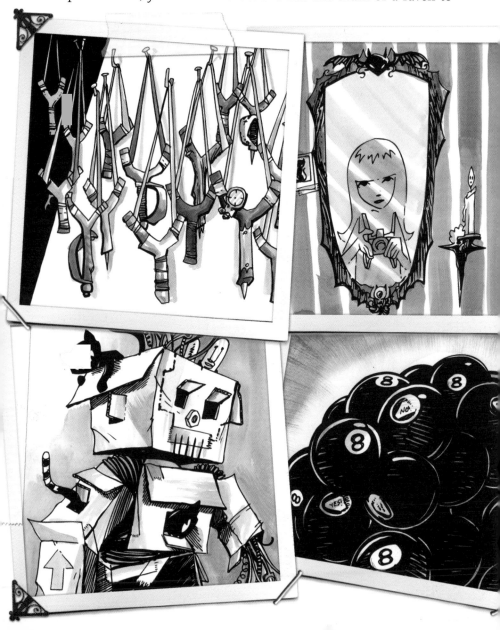

really get the joke, but still, the overall effect is EXCELLENT!!!!!
Am very pleased.

I may need to rethink keeping Raven in the birdcage. It's kind of highlighting her presence, and I prefer that she stay a little more under the radar. Back in Blandindulle, she'd mostly hang around the room, assisting with experiments or just sort of blending into the background. But here, in the cage, she's pretty much the first thing you notice. Um, by "you," I mean Mom, since she is the only human besides me who enters my room. She was up here just a few minutes ago to check out the décor but got completely distracted by Raven.

MOM: [To Raven.] Do you WANT to sit on that perch?

RAVEN: Uhhhhhh . . . yeah?

ME: It's performance art, Patti.

M: [Not really buying that.] E, tell me again about this person?

ME: Remember, I showed you her circuits? She's a raven. Robot. Android. Golem. . . . . It's fine.

M: I'd like to be supportive, but she gives me the creeps.

Then I was all proud and gave Raven a seedcake treat for being creepy. Have also gotten her out of the cage, just to please Mom.

Later

Consulted with Great-Aunt Millie on her attic. She has requested an all-white theme. Entire room will need several coats of paint. SIGH. If there's one thing I really don't get along with, it's white paint. Will be picking it out of my hair, fingernails, and clothing for a week. Should get Raven on this task. Should really get duplication device working and make some copies of Raven for faster attic-painting.

Later

Have been avoiding going to the store for white paint. Instead, spent a very fun hour frisking about the house with the cats. They have recovered from the indignity of the move and are thrilled with all the new smells, hidey-holes, unpacked treasures, and empty boxes. Personal territory has been sorted out, and Mystery is of course Mistress of the Bedroom. NeeChee is Ruler of the Netherworlds (AKA the basement). Miles has proclaimed himself Imperial Groundskeeper, and Sabbath ... well, Sabbath doesn't really have the personal authority to claim territory, but since no one else wanted the guest bathroom, it's pretty much his.

With the feline border disputes settled, we have collectively taken over the living room for the night. I cobbled together a cardboard Cat Maze—with strategic holes—and put Sabbath inside with some catnip. Then the other cats and I tormented him with paws, whiskers, and bits of string held just out of his reach until I hurt an internal organ from all the laughing.

Afterward, Sabbath got special snuggles to reward him for taking a hit for the team and being our laughingstock for the night. SOMEONE'S got to do it, and Miles, NeeChee, and Mystery have done their tours of duty over the years, so now it's Junior Cat's turn.

Anyway, I know he doesn't mind. He is not a cat of great dignity.

Later

Gobfarks! Cannot WAIT to get going on my Silifordville Master Prank. I definitely need to start now so I am not trying to throw one together during the last few days before we inevitably move again.

Unless a more brilliant plan presents itself, am sticking with my idea of duplicating everyone in town, then enjoying the chaos. Oh man. Had better start exercising abs now, so they can handle the gut-busting laughter.

Will just rest my eyes for a few minutes first. Am pooped from all the programming, unpacking, laughing, and interior decorating.

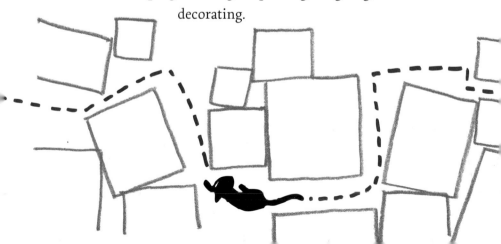

Later

Drool!!!!!

Just woke up, facedown in my journal. Have drooled all over the place. Going back to sleep.

June 3

sidewalks skated, 0; sewer tunnels explored, 17; personal mottos created, 1

OK—Silifordville is no Blandindulle, but it does have some superior sewers!!!!

It's always high priority with me, whenever we move to a new town, to check out the sewer system and its relative usefulness for my needs. The easiest place to get into the Silifordville sewers (that I've found so far) is on a dead-end street where all the buildings seem to be vacant or inhabited by invisible hermits—anyway, there was no one around to see me lift the manhole cover and sneak inside.

Of course I was wearing my special full-body sewer suit with oxygen tank—you only need to get bacterial pneumonia once, that's for sure!!

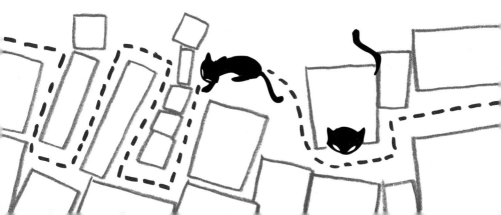

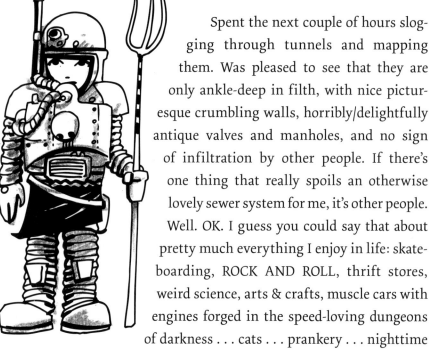

Spent the next couple of hours slogging through tunnels and mapping them. Was pleased to see that they are only ankle-deep in filth, with nice picturesque crumbling walls, horribly/delightfully antique valves and manholes, and no sign of infiltration by other people. If there's one thing that really spoils an otherwise lovely sewer system for me, it's other people. Well. OK. I guess you could say that about pretty much everything I enjoy in life: skateboarding, ROCK AND ROLL, thrift stores, weird science, arts & crafts, muscle cars with engines forged in the speed-loving dungeons of darkness . . . cats . . . prankery . . . nighttime loitering . . . the outdoors . . . the indoors . . . SOLITUDE . . .

Am making a new addition to my general philosophy of life. It goes a little something like this:

If there's one thing that really spoils [fill in blank with anything good], it's OTHER PEOPLE.

OK—enough philosophy for one night. Am now back at my original manhole and about to return to the surface. (Note: Original Manhole would be a great name for a band, if no other phrases were available.) Excellent progress for one night! Cannot wait to come back!

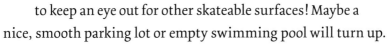

On the downside, there are no sidewalks in this town. Everyone parks their cars halfway up the lawns. Streets are too narrow and pavement too uneven for good street skating. Will have to keep an eye out for other skateable surfaces! Maybe a nice, smooth parking lot or empty swimming pool will turn up.

Later

On the upside, there is a tolerable junk shop in Silifordville, and as a little bonus it is next door to (and shares a Dumpster with) a hardware store! They may not keep late hours like Zenith did, but a Dumpster's doors are always open to a kid with lock-picking skills.

Later

May need to get Raven back in the cage after all!!!!

I think she must have overheard me telling Mom that I was going out to get to know the neighborhood. Anyway, when I got home from investigating Silifordville's sewers around one a.m., there was a police cruiser parked in front of our house.

SIGH! So soon, it begins . . .

Naturally I hid in some bushes to scope the situation. In a couple minutes the front door opened and a policeman left, politely saying good night to Mom. Once he was gone, I hurried inside to find out what the flagbrakes was going on. It wasn't good. Apparently Raven had taken it upon herself to go door-to-door introducing herself to the neighbors. From what Mom said, it went a little bit like this:

[Loud knocking.]

Neighbor: Yes? Is everything all right? Who are you?

Raven: Uhhhh . . . Raven.

N: Well, it's past midnight, Raven. What is it you want?

R: Uhhhhhhhhh . . . Iono?

N: Get off my porch, you!

So, yeah, after a few blocks of this, Officer Thomas came and picked her up. Am very glad that I sewed our address on her shirt yesterday. (Would have preferred to tattoo it on her arm but reflected that I would have to cross it out and update it every 13 months or so.) Am also REALLY FARBING THANKFUL that he didn't try any force on her, or there would be one badly broken police officer in Silifordville tonight. No, he just brought her home and gave Mom a talking-to about keeping her mentally slow daughter safe in the house, then (rather shyly) said she could always call him if Raven ever needed a personal escort around town.

WHEW!!!!

Not a great start for us in Silifordville, though.

Later

Raven and I have given the attic its first complete coat of white paint. UGH. We are both smudged and polka-dotted from head to toe. Wish I could take a bath in turpentine to get it all off me. Am hoping one more coat of paint will do it.

At least Great-Aunt Millie was appreciative and levitated Raven until it got me laughing.

Later

Have finished reassembling my lab and its command center, my lovely, lovely Oddisee—better than ever, thanks to Raven's help!

Am anxious to restart all my various projects. Duplicator and Master Prank are top priority, of course. Am looking forward to a summer full of weird science and prankery. Hopefully the science will lead to more effective prankery!!!

Also cannot wait to do more exploring, including closer surveillance of the neighbors, so I can learn their habits and weaknesses. Let the Summer of Silifordville begin!!!!!

June 4

Honking mugworts! Raven is causing more problems! Not sure exactly what got into her, but I suspect she is listening to my random comments to the cats about my plans and interpreting them as suggestions that she ought to act on. So anyway, during the day, while I slept, she wandered the neighborhood again, getting into random conversations, talking to birds, and generally weirding out the populace until the police brought her home. Of course Mom caught the worst of the trouble, as they started asking her hard questions about whether Raven wouldn't be better off in some kind of institutional setting where she could be looked after properly.

Anyhoodle. Mom has asked me to do something about Raven to prevent further family embarrassment. Am trying to figure out an acceptable solution. I mean, I worked hard on this round of programming, and it seems like such a waste to dumb her down again. And I NEED her to be smarter, to be a second set of hands for me. I've got a duplication device to build AND a Master Prank to mastermind! And I want to keep her. I mean, she's one of my greatest accomplishments, this little golem of mine.

The way I see it, Mom worries a bit too much about what

people think. Man, we've been over this soooo many times, like when the Blandindulle neighbors complained about my weird weed garden in the front yard, which, OK, to be honest, didn't exactly color-coordinate with the other gardens on the block and had been known to nibble on passersby.

Or like that time the Buttston school nurse decided I was being neglected, just because I always wear the same outfit. And Child Protective Services didn't even listen when I tried to tell them how lucky I am that Mom lets me wear what I want. Instead I had to see a shrink

KEEP OFF THE GRASS!
You've been warned!

about why I want to wear the same thing all the time. Lucky for me the guy was half asleep and incompetent. I bored him out of his head talking about science experiments, and after two sessions he told them I was perfectly well-adjusted. Mom and I laughed our cheeks off when it was all over, but, needless to say, I'm pretty sure she suffered all kinds of guilt and anxiety over that one.

Hmm, may need to work out some kind of compromise with Mom after all. Ugh, maybe later. Am itching to do some more Silifordville exploration.

Later—out and about . . .

Cats and I have done some preliminary patrols of the neighborhood, getting the lay of the land and scoping the neighbors. Got most of their names off mailboxes and have done some minor spying. Just need to know what I'm up against, in a general way.

Later

Morning—time for me to be in bed, but Mom needed to discuss the Raven Issue. I started off by telling her that I thought she'd been through enough on my behalf, and didn't need the neighborhood gossiping about my golem and asking pointed questions about whether Raven has a soul, and where I got the body parts I made her out of, and whether it might be appropriate to ask the FBI to come take a look at her.

Mom:	Yeah, well, I don't think anyone's going to ask THOSE particular questions, E.
Me:	Really? Then I guess we're good, right?
M:	Um, not really. First of all, if Silifordville is anything like Blandindulle, then half the men in town are going to have crushes on her within a week. And you know that's only going to lead to trouble.
Me:	Oh, right. Like, fistfights and stuff?
M:	[Rolling her eyes.] Yeah, and stuff. And what happens when I start getting the calls about my beautiful but slow-witted daughter, who's up on the neighbor's roof chatting with birds? How about when she accidentally puts someone in the hospital?
Me:	OK, Patti . . . why don't I just donate her to science? Would that solve the problem?
M:	Hey, no need to get sarcastic. I'm just saying, you brought her into the world, so you have to be responsible when she gets into trouble.
Me:	Hmph.

Am now upstairs pondering the problem. Am feeling crabby, as I always do when Mom wraps up discussions with pointed comments that are clearly meant to reflect on ME. But also . . . seeing her point.

Later—middle of the day

I should not be awake, but the household is in an uproar, and once again it is Raven's fault. Before I went to bed, I'd instructed her to spend the day cleaning up the house and yard. I mean, I was only trying to do something nice. How was I to know that Mom would step outside into what looked like a terrifying uprising of rotting animal zombies?

Yeah, so, I was awakened by horrific screaming and went down to scope the situation. Neighbors had gathered, Raven was covered in dirt, Mom was hysterical, and the yard was full of small skeletons, mummies, half mummies, and a few of your average bloated, putrefying carcasses.

I had to perform a little down-'n'-dirty detective work to determine whether there had been any foul play. It was fascinating, but all good things must come to an end eventually.

ME:	[Glancing up finally to see crowd of neighbors still standing around, looking horrified.] It's all right. I think it's safe to say that these birds, squirrels, snakes, lizards, possums, and raccoons died in the normal course of Nature.
NEIGHBOR #1:	[To Mom.] What's . . . wrong with her?
MOM:	[Nervously.] Nothing! She's just . . . scientifically minded!

Neighbor #2:	That stuff is like rilly gross.
Neighbor #3:	Man, do you really need to do . . . THAT . . . to a squirrel to know that it's dead?
Me:	[Staggering to feet. Lurching toward neighbors. Gargling slightly.]
Neighbors:	GAHHH! AIIIEEEEEE! [Dispersing. Very quickly.]

Mom was not super pleased at my Igor impression. It took several minutes of sweet talk for me to convince her that it was a funny joke and sure to improve neighbor relations in the long run. I also persuaded her that we can hardly blame Raven for not knowing that rotting animal bodies are an acceptable feature of a clean yard.

Mom made sure I clarified to Raven that rotting animals belong UNDERGROUND.

Raven corrected her mistake.

Am going back to bed.

June 5
incredible obstacle courses discovered, 1; incredible obstacle courses conquered, 0

Have been treed by a ferocious canine!!

The cats and I were working on a nice new set of covert paths through the neighborhood, and had made some great progress when we were thwarted by one of the nastiest dogs we have ever met!!! All we were trying to do was use his yard as a passageway between the O'Donnells' and the Kawamotos', and now he's acting like we want to destroy his precious food/owner/piles of poop/yarbles/whatever it is dogs care about. Am up in the tree right

DOGBEAST!

now, waiting it out. Hideous drooling dogbeast shows no sign of leaving.

While I'm up here writing, might as well take notes on the rest of what happened tonight, since it's actually kind of historical: I'd built a nice makeshift ladder on the O'Donnells' side so I could climb the fence, which really is unusually high; and then Mystery charged up it before I could even step on the first rung, so I let her do her thing; but when she got near the top, she slowed way down and her whiskers vibrated and she started hissing, which told me there was some kind of alarm system to disarm first.

So, this is a little bit embarrassing to write, but I actually

46

spent a good FIFTEEN MINUTES or so just LOOKING for the stupid alarm system, and when it didn't turn up, had to move on to Plan B and install some polythermal-shielded ceramic discs on the fence boards where I intended to make my entry. Luckily that did the trick, and I was over in no time.

I had just shimmied down the fence, and right away this massive slavering German shepherd/St. Bernard/grizzly bear was there threatening to amputate something for me. Cats bailed right away, and who can blame them? Luckily I'd had the foresight to tie a bungee cord around my waist and hitch it to a nearby tree, so I was able to scramble up out of reach of his ghastly snapping jaws without losing any precious flesh.

So, here I am, hanging out in this tree plotting my next move. The cats are standing in the O'Donnells' backyard looking up at me with their sympathetic "humans are awfully dumb" look, and I know they think I should give this one up and make us a nice safe route from the O'Donnells' to the Martins' instead. But I don't think I can let this yard go quite so easily. It's HUGE, and most of it seems to be an awe-inspiring obstacle course full of bizarre terrain and equipment. Get the dog out of the picture, and I could have a LOT of fun here.

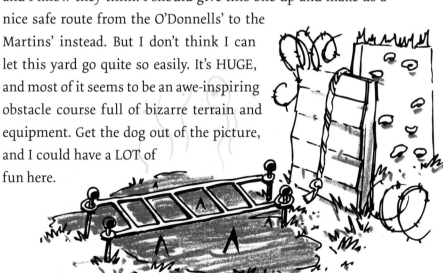

According to my notes from the other day, the name on the mailbox at this house is "Venus Fang Fang." For reals!!!!!! Cannot wait to see what SHE looks like.

Dogbeast is not leaving the tree. If anything, he is getting more frantic that I'm still here. Am a little concerned he may start barking and I will soon find out what Venus Fang Fang looks like when she's yelling at intruders.

OK. Am bungeeing to safety in the Martins' yard. Will come back when I have a plan.

Later—back at home

For once, Raven has not been up to any trouble while I was out and about, for the simple reason that I left her locked in the antique birdcage with a strict command not to leave it until I returned. I will just have to keep her caged from now on when I'm not around to supervise.

Have reflected that it's a good thing Mom can't (doesn't) keep ME caged when she's not around to supervise!

Later

Raven and I have finally (FINALLY) finished painting Great-Aunt Millie's attic white. I can't say I don't like it. Even if I prefer the attics we leave dark and dusty. This room has a certain expanding effect I don't really feel in my all-black, comfortably cluttered room.

Why white paint??? 48

Anyway, the best part is that it's DONE. YESSS! I can now get back to work on the duplication device. Have visited junk shop/hardware store Dumpster for supplies, unpacked radiac abrasive lightning rod, dismantled my Popsicle-stick prototype, and am now hard at work building Duplicator 2.0. Some progress, but not as much as I'd hoped. Have been sitting here running simulations on the Oddisee for a couple of hours, and I'm pretty sure I've figured out how to make good 3-D replicas of pretty much anything, as long as it's not alive. It's the little problem of duplicating living stuff that is still unsolved.

Am feeling very motivated to figure this out. This is going to be the most amazing Master Prank I've ever pulled off!!! Am also feeling the need to duplicate Raven. That way I can keep a spare hidden in our basement, in case something ever happens to the original. Would not put it past Silifordville to incarcerate my golem!

Later

Am being distracted from duplication project by funneee photos

49

coming through on the cat-cams. Here are a few of the highlights:

Later

Back on task. I managed to duplicate a tape-worm—sort of. The duplicate seems kind of flimsy and colorless, and disintegrates after a few seconds, AND is not actually alive, so I can't really call it a success.

Have asked the Magic 8 Ball a bunch of times what I'm missing, but so far the responses have run the gamut from useless to insulting: from "LENTILS" to "WHY IS A DUCK?" to "MISSING? LIKE A FOX!" Am somewhat demoralized. Daylight is coming. Drasty fladbax, I need a breakthrough!!!!!!!!

June 6
breakthroughs achieved, 0; skate "parks" discovered, 1; skate "parks" conquered, 1

Worked on the duplication project for a while, then decided I could use a

Sabbath thinks outside the box!!!!
AHHHAHHAHHAHAAAA!

change of scenery and some fresh evening air to help me think outside the box. (AHHAHHAHHAHAHAHAHHAH.) Cats and I have been tooling around Silifordville. Aside from its excellent sewers, it's really just your regular basic ordinary typical normal town. Small, but not remarkably small. It's got all the standard features a smallish town should have. The townspeople do not really deserve to have a sentence written about them, but here we are midsentence, so I might as well record that they are just your regular basic ordinary typical normal townspeople. SIGH! Boring.

Cats and I have given up the search for oddities, quirks, peculiarities, anomalies, and eccentricities in Silifordville and are now hanging out in a small park near the high school. The park features a basic half-pipe with a tight transition and not much flat bottom—rides kinda fast. And a couple stationary rails for grinding. Standard light graffiti. Crushed soda cans. Litterbugs.

Have skated the stuffing out of everything. Somewhat fun but also somewhat pathetic. It's been more entertaining just to sit on the bench with Mystery, watching the boy cats amuse themselves on the ramp and rails. Good times!

I have half a mind to bring some tools and lumber here tomorrow night and build improvements but am doubtful whether the local teens deserve this. Will probably do it anyway, since there are so few skateable alternatives in this town. (Note: Skateable Alternatives sounds like something I would have named a band . . . when I was like four.)

Later

Alarm! Alarm! I hear teens approaching in the distance. Am slinking into the bushes.

Later

Seven of your regular typical normal boring teens have arrived to skate their little park. I refuse to write another sentence about how standard, basic, average, and common they are.

—Oops.

Later

Had to resort to the sewers to get home without being seen by local teens. Did not have my sewer-diving suit with me and got home in an unspeakable state. On the upside, the stuff I scraped off my shoes and clothing has sparked a bit of a brainwave involving the jar of liquid black rock that I brought back from my ancestral home. I know that generations of scientists in my family used the stuff in all kinds of experiments, but until now it hasn't occurred to me (I blame the move) to try it in the duplicator project. Anyway, am getting down to work now. Will write more later.

LATER—OH MAN OH MAN OH MAN

UNBELIEVABLE NIGHT!!!!

I AM A SCIENTIFIC GENIUS!!!!!!!!!!

OK. Will slow down and start at the beginning.

That little brainwave on the liquid black rock was definitely what I'd been waiting for. Not that my success was easy. I tried this and that: dabbing the tarlike black rock on the transponder, spraying a fine mist of diluted black rock on the capacitor, hooking up an IV drip of black rock to the modulator, etc. And finally got my first good results: I soaked the motherboard in black rock, then hooked everything back up and turned on the power, flipped the switch, and BAM, I had TWO identical, living, squirming tapeworms instead of one.

Hopped around the room screeching with excitement and freaking out the cats for a bit, then made a few modifications and was about to try the device on Raven when the Oddisee's clock started to chime—which it hasn't done since I don't know when. Probably the last time there was a lunar eclipse or something.

And then my mirror, my big antique mirror that Mom says has been in the family forever, started to creak like it was going to fall off the wall. So I jumped up to go hold the mirror steady, which meant that I was standing in the duplicator's fieldframe when the clock chimed 13. And then Mystery got spooked, yowled, leaped onto the Oddisee, and was scrabbling around on it, so I reached over to shoo her off, and then CRASH the mirror went and fell on me. Glass everywhere, and I didn't dare open my eyes because there were shards in my hair. Finally got it all shaken out—looked up—and THEN I saw her—ME—HER!!

Long black hair . . . black dress . . . MY face . . . MY voice saying, "What the hagflax . . ."

But I wasn't talking . . . SHE was.

Time slowed down into weird split-second moments of wild emotions as the two of us stared at each other:

Moment of horror—

Moment of terror—

Moment of anxiety as I questioned my own sanity—

Moment of horror again as I thought about how I would explain this to Mom—

Moment of instinctive, protective, territorial rage that any other human had dared to enter MY room—

Moment of glee as I thought of all the cool pranks I could pull off with an identical twin—

ANOTHER moment of glee—

And then, "OK," we both said, and then we both started
laughing.

ME: Um, this is gonna sound dumb, but are you, by
any chance, ME?

OTHER ME: Uh, maybe. Emily Strange, right?

ME: Last I checked, yeah. Four cats, favorite color black, wicked bad? Etcetera?

OM: That's me all right. Hey . . . mind if I just . . . [Reaching out to me cautiously and pinching me on the arm.] . . . Wow. You're . . . real?

ME: Yeah. Are YOU?

OM: [Pinching herself on the arm.] Really Really Real, man.

ME: OK, what the jimjim happened?

OM: Oddisee chimed 13 . . .

ME: Then the mirror crashed on me . . .

OM: On ME . . . [Both of us starting to laugh again.] So, wow, it works! I CAN duplicate people!

ME: Great, who's next?

Then . . . it's a little embarrassing to write about, actually, but . . . I mean, I've certainly never done anything like this in my life, but I guess we were both kind of exhilarated about what had happened, and . . . OK. Let's just get right to it. We had a knockdown, bang-up, roll-around-on-the-floor GIGGLEFEST.

Right in the middle of the above-mentioned gigglefest, as the two of us were jumping like crazy on the bed and freaking the cats out and generally hyperventilating, Mom opened the door. I guess we didn't hear her knock, what with all the hysterical laughter. "Hey, E," she was saying, "sorry to bug ya . . . Sabbath's been eating something green, and it's all over the kitchen floor."

I bounced off the bed and was trying to catch my breath to introduce my twin when Mom spotted her still standing on the bed and promptly screamed a bloodcurdling scream.

Crabs! I rushed over and tried to calm her down and remind her what we promised the neighbors about screaming, but she was all like "AIIIEAIIEIIIAIIIEIIIE" and whipping her hands in the air like she does when she accidentally touches something dead, and the Other Me was sitting on the bed laughing like a crazy girl, and I could see the terror in Mom's eyes and her total inability to process what she was seeing, and I suddenly felt kind of panicked, and hustled her downstairs to have a chat.

ME: Patti, it's OK, it's really nothing to worry about.

MOM: Please tell me . . . it was a . . . hologram?

ME: Uh . . . no, she's really really real.

M: Cuz, E, you've done some pretty crazy stuff, I mean, it took me a while to wrap my mind around Raven being a . . . GOLEM, and I STILL have nightmares about her . . .

ME: Really? [Intrigued.] Good nightmares or bad nightmares?

M: [Starting to cry.] Emily . . . my nightmares are ALWAYS bad.

ME: Oh . . . sorry.

M: And that . . . girl upstairs? What is she, another golem, who looks like you, but has the mind of a . . . dead possum or something?

ME: Um, no . . . she's . . . actually . . .

M: —Don't say it—

ME: Me.

M: [Weeping freely.] No. Nope. Uh-uh, I can't deal with that.

ME: But Patti, just THINK what the two of us could accomplish together!!!!!!

M: [Horrified expression. Fresh outburst of hysterical sobbing.] But . . . but we just moved here and the neighbors already hate us and NOW YOU WANT TO TELL ME THERE'S TWO OF YOU?????

ME: Oh, so I'm that awful.

M: [Sniffling. Backpedaling.] Oh no, E, it's not that, you know you're the . . . uh, jewel of my existence and all, but . . . uh, it's just that having two of you may destroy me.

ME: Well, I don't know what else to tell you. You want me to say I'll go turn off the hologram machine and she'll disappear?

M: Yes, please.

ME: [Sighing. Wishing Mom could be excited for

me on the day of my greatest achievement.] Is
it enough if I just say you won't see her again?

M: . . . OK, but you gotta promise me on this one.

Me: Fine. I promise to pretend there's only one of me.

Cannot believe she made me promise. She never makes me promise.

Anyway, am now hanging out in the basement trying to put all this down on paper and get a grip on it. Am feeling another new emotion: mad at Mom. Believe it or not, have never in 13 years been mad at Mom. Reeeeeeally wish she could find the space in her brain to accept there being two of me. I mean, I'm ALSO having a hard time believing it's true, but in a different way. I keep worrying that I'll go back up to my bedroom to find out that Other Me has evaporated, or never happened at all.

I guess I could have tried to hide the truth from Mom, or make up some story instead of telling her straight out what happened, but it just didn't occur to me.

Interesting.

Anyway.

Will go find the Other Me and let her know the developments. And see if she wants a Raven for herself.

Later

Man! I reeeeeeeeally like having an Other Me around. Here are the top reasons so far:

1. She and I have both taken to calling each other "OtherMe," said quickly, so as to sound a little like "Emily." My First Nickname!!! (That I've liked. Much better than

   a. Halloween Girl
   b. Darkness
   c. Wednesday
   d. Doomsday
   e. Lilith Spookypants
   f. Deathily
   g. Vampira
   h. Freak
   i. Loner
   j. Riot Nrrrd
   k. Gothilocks
   l. Goth Moth
   m. Gothy McGothGoth.)

2. Can communicate essential ideas with a minimum of actual speaking.

3. Unlike conversations with other people, I don't actually mind speaking to OtherMe. Have already said more to her in our first few hours together than I've said to most people. Ever.

4. Work on science projects ought to go twice as quickly.

5. New possibilities in advanced prankery opening up.

6. Can finally, at last, TRULY be in two places at once. Lifelong dream come true!!!!
7. Perfect built-in alibi for future mischief.
8. Cats will now have all the human real estate they need for cozy nighttime snuggling and can knock off fighting over my warm spots.
9. Am enjoying strange and blessedly false sense of being "normal" because I'm "socializing."
10. Am enjoying seeing myself as if through someone else's eyes. Am pleased to say I am pretty much exactly as I should be.
11. Am looking forward to 50% fewer days spent in school.
12. Can now commence setting high scores on all my video games in cooperative mode.
13. Finally have a reason to avoid getting any hideous, scarring wounds to the face. Will start wearing protection when I work with hot splattering chemicals!

Later

Here is the Plan for Mom, as worked out by Me and OtherMe. It's so simple, it's downright Zen. We have hung up a sign on ~~my~~ our bedroom door reminding Mom to protect herself from what she obviously prefers not to see.

WARNING
DO NOT ENTER

DANGER OF EXTREME HORROR
AND MENTAL PAIN!!!!

IT'S A PROMISE!!!

OtherMe felt this should be enough on our part, but I reminded her of Mom's screaming hysterics, and we agreed that we will take turns leaving the bedroom, in the interest of family harmony.

We have also agreed to take turns on the Oddisee, since sitting in the same chair and trying to work on it simultaneously was NOT quite as harmonious as you might think it would be. OtherMe may be an exact duplicate of me, but she doesn't necessarily want to type the right-hand letters for me while we code.

Later

We have not been able to duplicate Raven, or tapeworms, or balled-up spiderwebs, or anything else. Looks like circuits took some heat damage during last duplication. Not to worry. We will work out the kinks and get Raven duplicated some other night.

Oddisee-Cam shot of Me and OtherMe!!

Later

Sun is coming up, but neither of us really wants to go to bed because we are having so much fun discussing fascinating topics like:

1. Do we have the same thoughts? (Pretty much.)

2. Can we communicate telepathically? (Would like to say yes. Truth is . . . not so much.)
3. Can we make AnotherMe? (Experiment pending; duplicator temporarily out of commission.)
4. What happens if one of us gets hurt—does the other one feel it? (After several fun and painful experiments, the answer seems to be no.)
5. What happens if one of us dies? (Experiment pending, ahhhahhaah.)
6. Will we look the same in a year? 13 years? 100?
7. If we go to school on alternate days, will we learn different stuff and grow into different people?
8. Do we want to grow into different people or stay the same?
9. What kind of different people would we want to grow into? (MANY very fascinating and creative answers!)
10. Assuming Mom eventually accepts us the way we are, will she like one of us more than the other?
11. What about the cats?
12. Where ARE the cats and why haven't they been upstairs all night?
13. Where do we go from here????????? (Rubbing hands together, much planning.)

June 7

Woke up about fifteen minutes ago, in the middle of the day, to find OtherMe wrapping me up in a rug. No, for real. And I'm glad I did all those experiments with liquid-liquid extraction last summer, cuz I knew right away I'd been drugged with ether.

Could barely croak out Raven's name. It's a frabbling good thing I built her with such sensitive hearing. She was there in a flash, and OtherMe jumped and dropped the rug, looking pretty disoriented.

OtherMe: What . . . where . . . who . . .

Me: [Croaking weakly.] What's going on, OtherMe?

OM: Hhhhh . . . hmmmm . . .

Me: Why am I in this rug?

OM: Why ARE you in this rug?

Me: Did you drug me with ether?

OM: No, I didn't drug you with ether. What, I'm gonna drug you with ether, as if you weren't MY OWN SELF? [Long pause as I asked myself the same question. And it seemed we both took a moment to consider question #5, above.] Sure . . . OK, yeah, I remember drugging you with ether. But it wasn't you, it was . . . uh,

hey, remember that golem I created, we created, last year, out of that decaying Tasmanian
devil? The one that didn't work out? The one that
tried to eat the cats, and took a swipe at Patti,
and smelled like putrid salami? The one we
had to drug with ether, and wrap in a rug, and
incinerate?

ME: [Not liking where this was going.] I remember
that one.

OM: Well, I was having this dream about that golem,
and in my dream I said to myself that I needed to
cancel the experiment. So . . . I guess that's what I
was doing. Um . . . sorry about that.

Raven had unrolled the rug/Emily burrito, and I was starting to
recover from the ether. I wasn't feeling super happy about all this,
or about the interruption to my nice nightmare about winning
the jackpot on the tickle-torture game show by outlasting all the
other contestants under the nefarious automated tickle-arms
of Gregor the Tickling RoboCockroach, or about the disgusting
smell of ether in my nose, or about the incredible headache the
ether left behind.

And I'm NOT AT ALL happy about the fact that OtherMe
might subconsciously see ME as an experiment, let alone an
experiment that might need canceling.

She apologized about sixty-six times and then went back to sleep.

Later

OtherMe feels super bad about the whole sleepwalking episode and has offered to let me have the entire night to myself in the room while she spends quality time with Mom. Sounds good to me!!

Am now feeling more sympathetic about the whole unfortunate sleepwalking business. Have had similar episodes in the past, like the time I dreamed that Sabbath asked me if we could go to the beach, so I put him in his cat carrier and strapped it to my skateboard. Turns out, I did this in real life as well as in my dream. We were halfway down the block when his yowls (and the pain of broad daylight) finally woke me up. Am hoping there are no further sleepwalking incidents, or at least none that threaten my life. Will spend the day working on some kind of apparatus to wake me if I am being rolled up in a rug and dragged to the incinerator.

Quite a bit later

Have completed a sort of headgear contraption I can wear while sleeping that will sound a gut-wrenching alarm if moved. SERIOUSLY gut-wrenching—I used sound waves that nauseate the human gut, thinking I would hardly get accidentally murdered if everyone around was vigorously vomiting. I (brilliantly) programmed a completely random code to disarm it—because, after all, OtherMe knows all of my usual passwords. Can't risk a sleepwalking episode that involves successful disarming of alarms!!

I now have my first official secret from OtherMe. I feel kind of bad about it, but it's all in the name of safety.

Just realized that I am ravenously hungry. OtherMe has obviously forgotten to smuggle up my food for the night. Will have to sneak downstairs and forage for myself.

Later

Am back with a sandwich I made very quietly in the kitchen while Mom and some of her new Silifordville acquaintances were sitting in the next room watching late night horror B movies. I snuck around behind the couch and ate my sandwich while eavesdropping. None of it was interesting except when Mom bragged to her friends about what OtherMe was out doing for the night, which involved a midnight shred at the skate park, a good rummaging through local junk-shop Dumpsters, and general unsupervised catting about town.

Man, that stuff sounds fun. And she told me she was going to stay in and spend quality time with Mom!

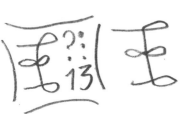

Am a little jealous.
Of myself.
How ridiculous!

Later

Am feeling unusually cooped-up in my room tonight, even though there are lots of lovely projects to keep me busy. Have already tried halfheartedly to get the duplicator working again. Lost interest after like 5 minutes and picked up the guitar instead. Played for maybe 7 minutes and put it down again. Tinkered with some modifications on my favorite slingshot—3 minutes. Then messed around with the Oddisee—13 minutes. Brainstormed Master Prank—2 minutes. Tried to psychically beckon OtherMe back from her nighttime jaunts—2 hours, 34 minutes. So far, unsuccessful.

Later

It's almost daylight, so I am going to bed. Still no sign of OtherMe. Have put on my protective headgear and set the alarm. Caught a look at myself in the mirror, and I can tell you, I look pretty special-needs with this thing on. The cats must have thought so too, because they all ran when I snuck downstairs to get them. Had to catch each one individually and tiptoe them up to the room, being careful not to wake Mom. Do not know WHAT their damage is tonight.

Headgear for my special needs. Let's hope I don't actually special-need it!!!!!!!!!

June 8

headgear alarms tested, 1; alarm codes forgotten, 1; eardrums bruised, 4

I woke up out of a lovely nightmare about sinking in licorice-flavored quicksand when the headgear alarm went off right by my ears. Just Like I Built It To Do. But I couldn't get it to stop because A) I didn't know who, where, or what I was; B) I couldn't think of the random code I programmed; C) OtherMe was kneeling on my arms, vigorously vomiting; D) I was vigorously vomiting. I tried my hardest to throw her off the bed, then realized we were both already on the floor. Friking vetbats! It's not that easy to wrestle someone who is exactly as strong and heavy as you are, AND is dreaming that you are some kind of Transylvanian mermaid intruder thirsty for her lifeblood, AND is covered in vomit. Raven had to pull her off me, pry apart the screaming headgear with a crowbar, and throw it out the window. Cats were all yowling and hissing. Lots of barf to mop up. OtherMe was extremely sorry. No one was pleased.

I may need to look into other sleeping arrangements.

Later—nighttime

It's my turn to leave the room. Finally!! Packed myself a sandwich and called for the cats, but I guess they are still freaked out by the headgear-alarm debacle, cuz they would not come near me. Am going downtown and undergroundtown to revisit the most interesting part of Silifordville—its sewers. Will write more later.

Later—around 2 a.m.

Amazing discovery—busted through to an unused region of the sewer system where the walls are like twelve feet high! Um, also, keyword = UNUSED. No idea what Silifordville built them for, but there has never been human poop sluiced through THESE tunnels. Nice!!! I discovered them while I was just slogging around beneath Silifordville, enjoying myself. Eventually I came to a dead end blocked by a watertight drain gate. I jimmied that gate right open, and there in front of me lay these beautiful tunnels—pristine, perfect, and ALL MINE.

I closed up the door behind me so that it can stay clean in here, and I've been walking around looking for a way to the surface. Nothing! I will have to make my own secret entrance, I guess. Will return with skateboard, cats, paint, brushes, snack treats, candles, Victorian tapestries, camera, surveyor's gear, mapmaking gear, and spelunking gear. OtherMe is going to be very impressed! CANNOT WAIT!

Later

Came back home to make sure OtherMe had sandwich provisions and found her at the Oddisee, coding away merrily, noshing egg salad. We spent the rest of the night working together on projects, all of which went much quicker with four hands. We cleared the floor in the back half of the bedroom and then started removing the floorboards, creating hidden compartments, and filling them with various treasures that we'll enjoy rediscovering when we move again. We drew up plans for an improved sun-spigot, similar to the prototype I built in the Dullton house, but with some nice modifications. And we increased the number of booby-trapped hidey-holes in the basement to seventeen.

And, very important, we built an interface we call the DreamSeizer™ that will allow the Oddisee to monitor OtherMe's dreams and wake her if she gets out of bed. Um, that's assuming she leaves the electrodes attached to her face all day.

Fingers crossed that we have a nice, uneventful day of sleep! I could use it.

June 9

tragedies narrowly averted, 1; mothers placated, 1; potentially regrettable decisions made, 1

Woke up shortly before sunset to find Raven standing beside the bed, holding an ax!!!! Oh bogflax, what a terrifying sight!

OtherMe was already awake, standing on the bed, struggling with Raven for control of the ax. I yelled at Raven to put the ax on the floor. Blasting dogfrix, am glad that ended well. We have no idea what she could have been thinking, but OtherMe said she heard me talking in my sleep, so clearly Raven was responding to that. OK . . . scary!!!!!!!!!! Am very glad that OtherMe was there to save me!

Anyway, OtherMe and I have talked it over and decided to follow through with our sarcastic threat to donate Raven to science. We'll miss her help around the lab, but as OtherMe put it, we're in a new town here, and we really want to be out and about, deep in exploration and espionage, not worrying about the mischief our golem is getting up to.

I did suggest other options.

ME:	We could just dial down her programming? Or lock her in the birdcage when we're not actually using her?
OTHERME:	. . . OK, look, I'll just admit it. I'm PROUD of Raven. She's AMAZING, and I made her out of bird parts! I want Science to know! Is that so wrong?
ME:	Uh . . . no, it's not so wrong. [Except . . . I think I'M the one who made Raven . . .]

Later

After much discussion with Mom, and several long phone calls, OtherMe has arranged for Raven to go live with Gigi Doubleton, President of the Silifordville Science Club. I argued for explaining Raven's true origins to Gigi, but OtherMe persuaded me otherwise, having cooked up the following very impressive pack of lies:

1. Raven was born in Eastern Europe and orphaned at an early age.

2. A very secret government organization adopted her, with the plan to turn her into some kind of superspy.

3. She was then subjected to years of hard training, hypnosis, experimental drugs, and radiation. (Go OtherMe!!!!!)

4. Her gentle spirit was completely broken by this rough treatment, and she failed to perform well on the spy SAT, or whatever they call it.

5. The secret government organization then smuggled her to this country and dropped her off at a rock festival, where they thought she would blend right in.
6. After being used as a sketchbook for the day by several tattoo artists, Raven wandered out to the parking lot and used her superspy lock-picking skills to break into Mom's car, where she fell asleep in the backseat.
7. Mom didn't even notice Raven in the car until they got home.
8. Having heard Raven's sad story, Mom decided to let her stay.
9. After a year of our warm, loving, supportive family environment, Raven has begun to heal. (AHHAHHAHHAHAHAHAHAAAAHHHH!)
10. What she needs now is a more science-oriented setting where her special needs can be addressed and her special talents harnessed.
11. Specifically, she has to be instructed to do everything. Otherwise, she is liable to sit around all day, not blinking or breathing, and giving everyone the creeps. (No lie.)
12. Also, she is not to be messed with, as she has the strength of 5 men. (Also not a lie.)
13. Also, she can talk to birds. (100% true.)

Surprisingly, Gigi Doubleton is very gung ho about taking Raven in, and apparently has elaborate plans for her rehabilitation. I guess I AM a tiny bit uneasy about all this, but OtherMe had some pretty convincing arguments, and Mom just looked so pleased to hear the news, and, hey, Raven's really a very sturdily built golem.

Anyway, I can always steal her back if necessary!

Later

Forgot to mention that our DreamSeizer™ interface for the Oddisee successfully captured lots of OtherMe's REM activity while we slept. And MAN!!!!! She sure has some icky dreams. No wonder she sleepwalks. Just as an example: In one of her dreams she suffered a hideous head wound that left her brain exposed. The cats accompanied her on the ambulance ride, but were tempted to their limit by the scent of raw, bloody brain. Cut to a scene of three cats licking their chops and one cat (Sabbath) licking the clean, empty interior of OtherMe's brainpan. And then her personality was divided among the four of them. Then the cats died, and their bodies were devoured by dozens of rats. Then OtherMe's and the cats' personalities were divided among them. Then the rats died, and their bodies were devoured by beetles. Then . . . yeah, see above.

I think it's safe to say this is weirder than my average weird dream. And when I told OtherMe I was kinda jealous of her weird dreams, she sorta cringed and said, "You can have them!" I guess she doesn't enjoy her nightmares like I do.

Poor OtherMe!!!!!!!

Later

It's OtherMe's turn to leave the room. She's going to do some scouting over at Venus Fang Fang's house. We have been coveting that amazing obstacle course and plotting a way to get the dog out of the picture. Here's hoping OtherMe comes up with something brilliant!

While she is out and about, I have decided to get myself reinstated in the cats' good graces. Not one of them has come near me in three days! I admit to feeling a little offended. Also, I'm kind of mystified. I mean, they've tolerated twelve moves, a raven-golem, and too many noisy/stinky/otherworldly science projects to count, and they can't deal with an extra ME? Zang, if anything, they should be stoked about getting twice the attention. Whatever. We will see what some snack treats, baby talk, and chin-scratching can accomplish.

Later

No dice!!! Am very insulted. Mystery saw me coming and turned tail—disappeared into the basement—I never did find her. Miles gave a bloodcurdling RrrrrrAowww and went out the window into the night. I managed to capture Sabbath and force him to endure a little petting, but I can only handle so much pain and blood loss, and had to let him go after a few minutes. Had the best results with NeeChee, who found himself cornered in my closet. He hunkered down and pretended to be asleep while I brushed, petted, and baby-talked him for a while. But the look in his eyes was sheer horror.

Am pretty devastated by this. I'm used to having my Posse around me (and on me and under me) all the time. They're the most perfect, intelligent, beautiful, sensitive, entertaining, hilarious companions I could hope for. And maybe it's not the healthiest attitude to prefer feline friends to human, but that's just how it is. They are my best friends, and suddenly they can't stand me, and IT HURTS.

Um, in fact, this is kind of embarrassing to write, but it actually made me start to tear up a little.

That's right! I said it! I cried. Do not even remember the last time I cried. Must win back my cats somehow and soon!

Later

OtherMe just got home. She says she went back to Venus Fang Fang's yard and tried to trap the dog in his pen with strategic use of leftover liver. (Leftover Liver = great name for a . . . well . . . for someone else's band.) He did not go for that.

OtherMe's new plan is to invent cat collars that will terrorize him into submission. The Posse can then infiltrate the yard for us and keep the dog under control while we enjoy the obstacle course. Told her I was all for that, but testing the collars might be tough, considering that the cats run from the sight of us.

this Band STINKS!

OTHERME:	Really? I hadn't noticed.
ME:	Seriously? You didn't notice three days of no cat affection?
OM:	Huh, no. Guess I've been thinking about other stuff. Like, you know, how I duplicated myself.
ME:	Yeah. [Except . . . I think I'M the one who duplicated myself . . .]
OM:	Just give them some snack treats and baby-talk them a bit. They'll come around.
ME:	Yeah. Thanks. I'll try that.

Am not real happy. Gah. Well, Mom's asleep, so I'm getting out of the house for a bit.

Later

Have cut a private door into the clean + dry section of the sewers through a convenient pothole I found (and enlarged) in the alley behind the junk shop in downtown Silifordville. Am very pleased.

Small drawback—hopefully small, that is: I was observed!!! I had finished crafting a nicely camouflaged door for my pothole, dropped down into the sewer, and started setting up my provisions for a good painting session, when I heard my door creaking open, and the next thing I knew, this kid had jumped down into the sewer and was standing around looking at my stuff!

I'm pretty sure I recognize him from the group of standard,

basic, average, common teens who interrupted my peaceful enjoyment of the local skate park the other night. (Then again, they all looked the same to me.) However, he may turn out to be somewhat less ordinary than most. I realize this violates the latest addition to my personal philosophy re: other people and their ability to spoil the Good Things in Life, BUT, he may be OK. I'm not completely sure yet. Our conversation went a little something like this:

KID: [Cheery. Annoying.] Hey!!!!!

ME: [Annoyed beyond words.] . . . . Nnnnnnnnnn.

KID: What's up, man, I saw you digging this hole, so I, like, hid and then I followed you down here! MAN, this place is rippin! Omigah, you got your brushes out, you're gonna paint down here, huh. Yeah, I been looking for a spot like this, some big empty concrete walls, maaaaannnnn . . . [Rubbing his hands across the walls like a freak.] These walls are PERFECT.

ME: Mmmm.

KID: Name's Larry, they call me Binary Larry, I write code on walls, big walls, in binary.

ME: That's kind of counterproductive.

BL: Yeah, well, that's what they all say, they just don't get it is what I say, they don't see the beauty, the cold and gorgeous beau—

ME: Counterproductive's not a
        bad thing.

BL: Oh wow! You DO get it! You
        totally get it, man. Hey, so like,
        what's your name?

ME: [Turning away. Mumbling as
        much as possible.] Mmmlee.

BL: Emily. What a great name. So,
        yeah, Emily, is it cool if I come
        down here and write code? I
        could, like, take the south-
        and west-facing walls, and
        you could take the north-
        and east-facing walls?

ME: [Enduring terrible, invisible
        struggle inside: Dislike for
        Humanity vs. Loyalty to Fellow
        Coder and Painter.] [Grudgingly
        allowing the latter to win.] [Nodding.] K.

BL: Woohoo! Yeah, Em, it's gonna be so slickin!!
        I'll bring my boom box, and some music, and
        burgers, and—

ME: WHOA, WHOA, WHOA, WHOA. Couple of things
        we need to get straight.

BL: [Totally chastised.] OK?

Me:	[Ticking off items on my fingers.] You can never call me anything but Emily. You cannot bring burgers into my sewer. If your music sucks, and it probably does, I'm turning it off. And you will never again say "Woohoo."
BL:	Dude. I'm so checked. I'll never say that horrible word again. See you tomorrow night, man!!!!

Yeah, I'm pretty ambivalent about letting this Binary Larry back into my sewer . . . but, BUT, he appears to be willing to learn from his mistakes, and well, criping thujones, all the kid wants is a place to WRITE BINARY ON WALLS, and I can kind of appreciate that.

Yeah. I may regret this. We will see.

Later

Have made some progress getting the sewer ready for extended painting sessions. Have constructed cat ladder so that the Posse can come with me tomorrow night. Assuming they like me tomorrow night.

Cannot wait to show this place to OtherMe!

Later

Back at home. Have decided that sharing a bed with OtherMe is a bit too close for comfort, what with the sleepwalking and the creepy dreams and the accidental doses of ether, so I have rigged myself a cozy hammock near the ceiling, with a rope ladder I can pull up after me. It's not like I don't trust her, and it's not like I think she would, I don't know, intentionally remove the electrodes from her face so that I can't tell when she's left the bed during the night, but . . . well, let's just say I enjoy my nightmares better when I'm not concerned about ACTUALLY getting accidentally murdered in my sleep, OK?

June 10

golems donated to science, 1; possible horrible mistakes made, 1

Note to self: Do not ever, <u>ever</u>, <u>EVER</u> join the Silifordville Science Club!

Gigi Doubleton, President, and her sister Bebe, Vice President, came over after dinner to have some coffee and pie and meet Raven. OtherMe was hiding out in the bedroom.

GIGI: So this is young Raven. We've heard so
          much about you, dear.
RAVEN: Uhhhhhh?
ME: She doesn't talk much.
G: Well, we'll certainly work on her
          conversational skills.
ME: Con-ver-sa-tion-al skills. So . . .

hm . . . what kind of scientists are you, anyway?

MOM: [Laughing nervously.] Sorry, my daughter doesn't mean to be rude, but she's VERY interested in science. I'm sure she'd love to know your specialties.

BEBE: Oh. Ha ha ha ha ha ha ha ha ha ha! We're not SCIENTISTS.

G: Raven, dear, why don't you say your goodbyes, and we can show you your new home? Ms. Strange, lovely to meet you, no time for pie, we have SO MUCH shopping to do, and I can see that Raven desperately needs a complete spa treatment . . .

MAN!!!! Those are some annoying, self-satisfied, stuck-up, self-centered, non-science-oriented ladies. I have no idea why they decided to form a Science Club when they are clearly not interested in science. Unless you count the science of accelerating the drying time of nail polish (Wave Your Hands in the Air vs. Use a Blow-dryer?), the science of choosing your

Gigi and Bebe!

lifelong hairdresser, and the science of marrying a doctor.

Needless to say, I immediately formed an intense dislike of them based on their clothing, perfume, posture, names, facial expressions, and voices. Maybe that's unfair of me, but I had expected them to be much more academically oriented and much less obsessively well-groomed.

Anyway, I now understand why they are so interested in taking Raven in. It turns out that Gigi and Bebe had already heard quite a bit of town gossip about her. Surprisingly, the town gossip has nothing to do with her being a preternatural creature possibly made of undead body parts, and everything to do with her being beautiful, mysterious, and shabbily dressed. Man, I really don't understand people ~~sometimes~~ at all. Anyway, the Gige and the Beeb see her as a diamond in the rough, and plan to get her polished up, so that she can be the social hit of the season and make them wildly popular. Or something like that. Secretly, I suspect them of wanting to use her as bait for attractive gentleman doctors.

They did not even stay to hear any of my tips on Raven care and maintenance, but gathered up "their" Raven and hustled her away. Gah!!!!! Have taken note of their address, in case I need to bust her out. Who knows, maybe as soon as tomorrow!

Later

Could not wait for tomorrow. Am sitting in the bushes outside Gigi and Bebe's house. Wow, I kind of didn't realize a town this small could hold houses this big. They are RICH! And Raven is clearly getting the best of care. I spied on Gigi and Bebe for a while as they gave her some sort of makeover. It was highly entertaining. I mean, I'm pretty sure these ladies have never done their own nails in their lives, but there they were, down on the floor, giving Raven a pedicure! Good stuff. I guess I can let them have their fun for a while and give Mom a break from golem stress. Have scoped out their security system, and it will be at most two minutes' work for me to disable, should the need come up.

—Gotta get home, am expecting a phone call—

Later

Back at home. Have received the expected phone call from Gigi, asking how we get Raven to do things. I couldn't resist having some vengeful fun with her.

ME:	What do you want her to do?
GIGI:	Well, at the moment I want her to go upstairs, but she just stands there.
ME:	Oh, right. Well, here's the thing about that, see. She's programmed only to respond to me.
G:	Sorry? I don't understand. You're referring to her spy training, I suppose. Some kind of brainwashing, perhaps?
ME:	Sure, whatever.
G:	Well, I would appreciate it if you'd tell me how I

can get her upstairs.

ME: Well, luckily for you, I inserted a special code word in her programming when I built her.

G: BUILT her? I'm sure you're . . . Hmph. Is your mother there?

ME: Sorry, she's really busy exfoliating right now.

G: Just tell me the word, young lady.

ME: "Jockstrap."

G: The word is "jockstrap"? I say "jockstrap" and she'll do as I ask?

ME: [Holding in the laughter. Holding it in, holding it in.] Oh . . . sorry, no, try "poopcake."

G: "Poopcake." Raven, please go upstairs. No, it's not working.

ME: [Holding it in . . . barely . . .] Um, try "barfbag." [And so it went, through "Titicaca" and "codpiece," to "Mulva" and "Dolores," to "dissemination" and "kumquat," until I completely lost it, and had to put the phone down for a few minutes while I caught my breath.]

ME: Sorry about that, I had a bit of a . . . coughing spasm. [Spasm!! Ahahhahhahhha!]

G: Let's stop this nonsense right now. Either give me the word or put your mother on the line.

ME: Yes, ma'am! Seriously, the word is "Emily."

G: Raven? "Emily!" Please go upstairs. All right, that

worked. Now, good night to you, young lady.

ME: And good night to you, Gigi. Thanks for the laughs.

G: Hmph!!!

Later

Was very energized by belly-busting laughs at Gigi's expense, and rallied OtherMe to help me tackle some projects. Am happy to report that we have just finished work on a small, but serviceable treehouse in one of the ginormous trees out back. It's the eleventh treehouse I've (we've?) built, so I/we are pretty much treehouse experts by now, but this time it only took three hours, eleven minutes—three full hours faster than my/our record! We were both especially pleased at our success in completely camouflaging both the treehouse and the ladder up to it—there's pretty much no chance of any stray neighborhood child accidentally seeing it from the ground. We equipped it with some basic booby traps just in case.

Later—another project down!

We have finished the sun-spigot! It is excellent! The solar panels collect sunlight all day. Then it gets condensed and stored in a tank in the bedroom. We've rigged up a hose and spray gun so that every night we can hose down the plants with super concentrated sunlight. We also made two totally sunproof suits so that we are not scorched by toxic sun. As much as we love and

respect plants, it's a mystery to us how they can stand that stuff. Anyway. What's important is that we were able to bring all our bizarre, beautiful plants up to our room and now have a huge crazy garden up here. At last! Let the crossbreeding begin!

Later—incredibly productive night!

We have created cat collars with sonic dog-repelling devices on them. Am wearing mine around my ankle and roaming the neighborhood a bit, looking for dogs. Will report back in a bit.

Later

Back to the drawing board. The dog repeller also repels cats, squirrels, rats, birds, reptiles, and insects. All around me, in my peripheral vision, I can see animals running, flying, crawling, or squirming in terror to get away from me. Unacceptable. I am already feeling enough animal rejection at home!

Will keep it for sewer use, however.

Later

Am exhausted from super high productivity of the night. Am thrilled to have OtherMe here to make projects go so quickly. Am climbing into my hammock for some sleep.

Later—in the hammock

Just realized I forgot to tell OtherMe about my secret sewer. Let alone visit it. Oh well, she is already asleep. Maybe tomorrow.

Binary Larry better not have been up to any teen-style lameness down there, or he will PAY!!!!

June 11

Town Halls cased, 1; super elaborate Master Pranks conceived, 1

Man, I'm sooooooooo into having an identical Me around. Tonight was pretty much the best night of my life, mainly because OtherMe and I spent several hours laying our plans for what is going to be a pretty stupendous prank on the town. Or is it even a prank? I think it's more a work of art. It'll take a few days to set up, but it'll be sooooooooooo worth it.

I was still feeling very gung ho on the whole "Duplicate Silifordville" idea, but OtherMe has come up with a far superior concept. She heard on the news that there's going to be a ribbon-cutting ceremony at Town Hall next week—for what, she doesn't know or care. What matters is that a big crowd of local people will be there, and that's all the inspiration she needed.

We waited until Mom was fast asleep, then snuck out of the house together and spent a few hours exploring Town Hall and the adjacent grounds. Man, I should have checked out the place more closely before this! I would have immediately added it to my short (Very Short) list of Good Stuff in Silifordville.

Here are some of the wonderful things Town Hall had to offer us:

1. Large statues of anatomically correct naked folk.
2. A bench with a commemorative plaque reading: "IN LOVING MEMORY OF RITARDO N. O'BRANE, FOUNDER OF SILIFORDVILLE."
3. Several achingly beautiful, pristinely white, longing-for-the-spray-can walls.
4. An outdoor exhibit of log cabins.
5. Playground populated by huge, colorful, plastic, easily unbolted barnyard animals.
6. A rooftop garden.
7. Indoor bird and rodent life.
8. Janitorial staff mostly under 20 years old and easily distracted from work responsibilities.
9. A supply closet and toolshed with locks a 2-month-old could crack.
10. Transom window leading to the storage room

where they keep the uniforms. Uniforms!!!!
11. Large, antique, dusty, unused heating ducts that lead into every room.
12. A perfectly round library with a retracting roof.
13. An empty Olympic-sized swimming pool.

With all those possibilities, we had no choice but to discard them and do something completely original and self-sufficient. OK, well, actually we did use the heating ducts as passageways in our travels, which felt gloriously covert and spylike. And man, I loooooooooooove bumming around in the empty Town Hall at night with OtherMe! After thoroughly casing the joint, we took over the boardroom for a planning session.

SO. Here is OtherMe's big plan: We're going to create a wondrous Manifesto that will open people's minds to the beauty of Strange, and then modify the town's A/V equipment so it is capable of projecting our Manifesto directly into their brains. Then on the night of the ceremony, once the crowd has gathered, we'll seal the doors and roll the Manifesto. Everything will be remotely controlled

before: BORING

after: STRANGE

from the safety of our bedroom. Then we just sit back and watch the town of Silifordville get STRANGE!!!!!!

YESSSSSSSS! Here's to OtherMe and her rascally diabolical plans!

OK—pretty great progress for one night. We are headed home.

Later

Am wondering about OtherMe. We were hanging out in the treehouse, and for a long time she was staring through the binoculars and laughing her cheeks off. I finally asked her what was so funny. She showed me where to look: Venus Fang Fang's backyard, where her dogbeast, in obvious distress and agony, was throwing himself at the back door. A woman I assume was Venus Fang Fang herself would occasionally come to the window and stare out at him, looking bewildered.

ME: What's so funny about that?
OTHERME: I threw my dog repeller into Venus Fang Fang's yard.

Me:	[Staring at her. Wondering if she had gone insane.] Why would you do that?
OM:	[Staring at me. As if wondering if _I_ were nuts.] Um, for fun?

Varking hamdacks! Am now sitting outside Venus Fang Fang's backyard preparing to reinstall the polythermal-shielded ceramic discs on her fence, climb over, and remove the dog repeller. Am somewhat surprised that I am willing to risk my personal safety for the comfort of the dogbeast, but his yelps of anguish are truly haunting. Cannot just sit around while an animal is being tormented.

Hope he sees me as his rescuer from suffering, and I come out of this with all my limbs!!!!

Later—hiding in some bushes

Am real grumpy. Was confronted by Venus Fang Fang. She is obviously not the person who built the supercool obstacle course in her backyard.

She has a sour temper, a peculiar accent, and a strong hatred for anyone caught on her property. Our conversation went a little bit like this:

Venus Fang Fang

VENUS FANG FANG:	Chald! What are yao daoing in ma backyard?
ME:	[Her accent grating horribly on my ears.] Ugh! What? Oh. Just . . . getting my cat collar. Be out of here in a flash.
VFF:	And haow dad yao gat in haere?
ME:	Climbed the fence.
VFF:	[Shooting poison glance around perimeter of fence. Zeroing in on my polythermal-shielded ceramic discs. Stalking over to them and snatching them down.] Indaeed. Ah'll be aover to spaeak with yaor mather in the marning.

Crabs! Am not pleased. OtherMe owes me big-time for this. Am heading underground for some peaceful art-style self-therapy. Am NOT bringing OtherMe. And Binary Larry had better go easy on the cheerful conversation. Am in no mood for it!!!!!

Later

Am hanging out in the lovely sewer, prepping a few north- and east-facing walls for a grand sewer mural. (Sewer Mural = great name for a band.)

SEWER MURAL

Binary Larry got here shortly after I did, but I managed to snap a photo of his insanity/art before he arrived.

Later

Am feeling better. Art-style self-therapy is GOOOOOOOOOOOD! Am heading home to bed.

June 12

neighbor altercations slept through, 1; mothers distressed, 1; doppelgängers paying for it, 0

Was just woken from a lovely nightmare about rolling around from one thundercloud to another, getting zapped with painful bolts of lightning, by Mom knocking at the door. OtherMe hid herself in the blankets as I went to answer it.

ME: Mornin', Patti.

MOM: So, I hear you disarmed Mrs. Fang Fang's alarm system and snuck into her yard?

ME: [Wishing I could just tell her, "IT WAS THE OTHER ME!!!"] Yep. But I was on legitimate business. Fetching a cat collar.

M: Couldn't you have just knocked on her door and asked for help?

ME: . . . . No.

M: [Sighing.] Well, if that's how it is, you'll have to deal with the consequences.

ME: What consequences?

M: Mrs. Fang Fang would like you to walk her dog, Viscer, once a day for the next week. And look, do me a favor, E. Don't let me hear about any more trouble with THAT character. Her accent is brutal.

Me: Indaeed.

M: Seriously, she seems like the suing type. And . . . I don't know . . . I'd just like for there to be ONE town on earth where the neighbors don't fear and/ or loathe us. K?

Me: You got it.

M: [Handing me my polythermal-shielded ceramic discs.] [Sighing.] [Leaving in silence.]

Am going back to sleep. Hope I dream of a nice, efficient way to get some payback from OtherMe.

Later—nighttime at last

OtherMe woke me up at nightfall with some truly awful guitar playing. Was giving her the benefit of the doubt for the first five minutes or so, and pretending to myself that she was playing some like really advanced space-jazz-skronk-noodling, but as the moments passed, and her curses got more creative, I realized that she really can't play the guitar.

Curious!

Am now feeling bad that I wrote such mean- spirited things about her. Still, SHE'S going to be walking that dog.

Mystic
Mystery
Mysterious
Mysteriouser!

Later

OtherMe was surprisingly agreeable about walking Viscer and has just left to go over there. As a very mild payback, I told her nothing about Venus Fang Fang. Ahahhahhah. Dogwalking + Venus Fang Fang . . . should make for a hilariously aggravating session! Cannot wait to hear her report.

Also, as soon as she stepped out the door, I picked up the guitar to see if I had also somehow lost my skills, but a howling rendition of "Blood Gets in Your Eyes" has proven I am as virtuo-spastical as ever. Curiouser and curiouser!!!!!

Later

Have tinkered with the duplication device—3 minutes. Attempted an overhaul of the Oddisee's memory backup devices—12 minutes. Started to reorganize music collection using an elaborate system of color-coding—6 minutes. I have serious attention deficit tonight. REALLY want to get out of the house, but Mom already saw OtherMe leave to walk the dogbeast . . . and I DID promise not to hurt her mind with evidence of our duplication . . .

Am sneaking out the window and heading down to the sewer.

Later

Gabfrax. Not so sure about Binary Larry right now. He was hang-ing out writing his epic code until around midnight. Have never met anyone so squirrelly. The one thing I cling to is that he is not nocturnal like me, though he thinks he is. In fact, we had the following discussion about it:

BINARY LARRY:	Yeah, so, I been coming down here every night since that first night, it's really great, I really can't sleep at night, you know, there's just too many thoughts. Are you like that too?
ME:	What, manic-psychotic?
BL:	Hahaha, no, man, I mean nocturnal!!!
ME:	Oh. Yes.
BL:	Man, do you ever wonder why there isn't a word for the opposite of nocturnal? I mean, what would that even be, like, "un-nocturnal"? Wow!
ME:	Um, there IS a word for that. It's "diurnal."
BL:	Nooooooo . . . waaayyyy! What does that even mean?
ME:	[Sighing.]
BL:	Oh . . . right.

Anyway, he eventually rolled out when his true diurnal nature kicked in and he could not keep his eyes open. I should be able to avoid him most of the time, as long as I show up after midnight.

Documentation of my progress on the mural.

Later

OtherMe says she has nothing special to report about her dogwalking episode. That's right. Nothing . . . Special . . . To . . . Report. Interesting. Anyway, we are heading over to Town Hall now for some quality work on our Manifesto prank. Will write more later.

Later

Shellac!!! Am in lots of pain right now! I bailed out on the skateboard, hard. No bones broken. Not much skin broken. Some bruising. Ego somewhat crushed. Feelings slightly hurt when OtherMe ran to pick up the skate before checking on me. When she saw my look, she was all like, "What, I knew YOU were OK." But STILL, give a girl the courtesy of checking on HER first, before you pick up the SKATEBOARD, right????

Must shake it off. Visualize the lovely sewer mural. Imagine still, calm, beauteous pools of liquid black rock. Think of the magnificent Master Prank. Reflect on the eyes that will be opened, the souls that will be freed from their Chains of Normalcy by the glorious Manifesto of Strange!

OK, am feeling better.

Later

Lots of good progress tonight. Spent several hours down in the basement of Town Hall, in the isolated room where the footage for the public-access channel gets reviewed and edited. And we completely raided that lovely library of archival footage. We cobbled and spliced and voiced-over the footage, and then painted liquid black rock right onto the film, until we had the beginnings of a beautiful, moving, inspiring **Manifesto of Strange**.

You know how, when you see a horror movie featuring an Especially Strange Person, the protagonist (who is never the E.S.P.—an E.S.P. can only be an antagonist, according to the movies) must always discover some dark artifact from the E.S.P., some painting or film or scrawled notebook or wicked shrine of newspaper clippings, that hints at the extreme Depth and Horror of their Strangeness. Right? Except that the dark artifact itself, in the horror movie, is never really very Deep or Horrific, and you kind of just have to accept that all the filmmakers could do was hint at the true Depth and Horror, or risk driving their audience to madness. Well—this Manifesto of Strange that OtherMe and I made is the REAL STUFF, MAN! No one, I mean no one, I don't even care how normal they start out, will be able to resist it. This town is going to be soooooo strange in three days' time. Cannot wait to see it.

(By the way, Dark Artifact = great name for a band.)

Before we left, we snuck from one conference room to another and started modifying the A/V equipment as we went, so that each projector or PA system will be able to work as a module that can be easily plugged into a central unit in the main auditorium to become an integrated, multi-lamp, multichannel, multispeaker, three-dimensional projector.

One more night of work on the Manifesto, and it'll easily be the strangest work of art ever projected guerrilla-style into the minds of unsuspecting attendees at a ribbon-cutting ceremony in any small town, anywhere. Yesssssssss!!!!!!!

Later

OtherMe and I returned home, high on life and ready to take on the world, or at least some weird science, and now, just two hours later, we are sitting around in ~~my~~ our bedroom, using a complete and working cat translator!!!!! . . . Actually, all exclamation points aside, I should say that it's kind of a letdown. I mean, I already know what the cats are saying, and it doesn't sound as great in English. Cats are a lot like French people—for many reasons, one being that everything they say sounds much cooler in their language.

In any case, here's what they've had to say:

1. Let us out! (constantly, by all of them)
2. Now! Now! Now! (constantly, by all of them)
3. Where is my catnip? (several times, by Miles)
4. Why are there two of you? (many times, by all)
5. I dislike there being two of you. (mostly Mystery)
6. I will punish you for this. (Mystery)
7. Mystery has defiled the closet. (Sabbath—that tattletale)
8. Let us do as Mystery has done. (Sabbath, NeeChee, and Miles)

9. What is that shiny thing on the other side of the room? (Sabbath)
10. Don't touch me. (every time I tried to pet one of them)
11. Put me down. (every time one was picked up)
12. You will pay for this in your own blood. (see above)
13. &*%^$&#$%&$ (frequently—man, who knew cats had such filthy mouths?)

Am feeling proud of us for completing the translator but annoyed at the cats for not being more pleased that there are two of me. They will just have to get used to it!!!!!!

Later—just before daybreak

Mom was reading the paper at breakfast when she suddenly started cackling. "Hey, E," she said, "your, uh, friend Raven made the Silifordville paper!" We had a good hahaha together over the headlines ("Local Birdbrain Wows Scientists, Suitors") and the photos (Raven demonstrating feats of strength and communication with birds; Raven posing with the ladies of the Silifordville Science Club; Raven fending off suitors with judo).

But since then I have been sitting here feeling very displeased about Raven being exploited by the ladies of the Silifordville Science Club. Had thought that they were going to shelter her from the world a little better than this.

Told OtherMe about the episode and suggested we bust Raven

out and bring her back home, but OtherMe brought me to my senses.

> OTHERME: What are you, dull? Remember that little incident with the ax?
>
> ME: Well, yeah, but it's not like she'll do THAT again.
>
> OM: C'mon. You don't HEAR yourself talking in your sleep, man.
>
> ME: Really, it's that bad?
>
> OM: For serious. You're all like, "Mrble mrble oh no the nefarious arms of Gregor the Tickling RoboCockroach are slaughtering me mrble mrble mrble."

ME:	Ahahhahahhhahah! Well, that doesn't sound too dangerous.
OM:	And then you're all like "DESTROY THE ODDISEE!" and then you're all like "CUT MY HEAD OFF WITH AN AX, RAVEN!"
ME:	OK, that DOES sound serious.
OM:	"MRBLE MRBLE RAVEN, YOU MUST KILL MYSTERY AND PATTI!"
ME:	[Shocked.] OK! I get the picture.

Vardtrax!!!!! Did not realize I had ~~so much~~ ANY subconscious hostility toward Mom and Mystery. Am grateful that OtherMe is looking out for us. Will not raise the subject of Raven again!

Later

In hindsight, it might not have been super tactful of me to bring up the whole losing-her-guitar-skills thing to OtherMe. All I said was, "Hey, OtherMe, was that a new musical genre you were inventing earlier, or do you just suck at guitar now?" She got steamed, made some cutting remarks about my performance on the skateboard, and left in a huff. Looks like she's going to sleep in the treehouse.

Not used to sleeping alone anymore. Sure wish OtherMe would come back inside. I feel kind of . . . lonely, I guess that's what that feeling is. Not an emotion I have felt too many times in my life.

June 13

Master Pranks threatened, 1; mothers and identical twins cooperating with me, 0

Mom is being difficult tonight. She wants me to go with her on our annual fun family outing to Black Basin Canyon tomorrow, which ordinarily I would love to do, but right now OtherMe and I have a Master Prank to pull off. Have not yet come up with a convincing story to get us out of it.

Later

Unbelievable!! OtherMe has broken my promise to Mom. Here's what happened: I had told OtherMe that we needed a story for Mom to get me out of going to Black Basin with her, and OtherMe was all like, "I'll handle this," and ran downstairs. Naturally I eavesdropped on their conversation—I didn't bug all the rooms in this house for nothing! Here's how it went:

OTHERME: Dude, Patti, we gotta reschedule that family outing.

MOM: But tomorrow's the new moon, and you know that's the best night of the month to go.

OM: Well, it's kind of important. The other Emily and I have to be here to pull off the final step in this huge elaborate prank we've been cooking up for the last few days. If we don't, well, you can imagine what it'll do to our self-esteem.

M: [Sounding weird.] The . . . other . . . Emily? Is that what I heard you say?

OM: [Annoyed.] Come ON, Patti. You know what's going on and it's time you faced up to it.

M: [Sounding unstable.] So, you're asking me to accept that you . . . "duplicated" . . . yourself during an experiment?

OM: That's exactly what happened. Is that so hard to understand?

M: [Getting slightly hysterical.] I thought YOU understood . . . that I don't WANT to understand! I thought we had an agreement! YOU PROMISED!

OM: Get over it, Patti! There's two of me now! You have TWO . . . IDENTICAL . . . DAUGHTERS!!!!!!!

M: [Crying. Running to her room.]

Am extremely peeved with OtherMe! She is responsible for my first fight with Mom! (Wait . . . is it even MY first fight with Mom? Very confusing.) AND she broke our (my?) promise. Am going to confront her as soon as she gets back up here.

Later

Am hiding out in the treehouse. Have had my first fight with OtherMe. Ugh! Here's how it went:

ME: DUDE! You broke our promise to Mom!

OTHERME: Hey, I'm not the one who made that stupid promise.

ME: But . . .

OM: That's right. Make all the lame promises you want. Makes no difference to me.

ME: But . . .

OM: Look, Patti needs to get tough with herself and face the truth, that's all.

ME: Stop calling her Patti.

OM: [Snorting.] You do, all the time.

ME: Only to her face.

OM: Man, how'd you get to be such a baby? Whining, complaining, picking your nose, tiptoeing around Patti . . .

ME: And how'd YOU get so evil? Breaking promises? Tormenting Mom's mind?

OM: Get over it. We've got work to do. I need you to help me finish the editing on the Manifesto and move all the projectors into the central auditorium.

GRRR!!!

Am feeling very let down by this whole self-duplication thing. Am actually wishing it had never happened at all.

Also, did not really realize it until now, but there HAS been a drastic increase in the time my finger spends up my nose. Very strange. Do not like the fact that OtherMe has noticed. Will try to control myself.

Later

OtherMe and I pushed our drama aside for the moment and went to finish our work at Town Hall. I let her handle the editing—I didn't feel like being in that small room with her tonight—while I went from one conference room to another, collecting the modified A/V equipment and plugging it into the central unit in the main auditorium. I didn't even bother to use the heating ducts like we'd started off doing. It suddenly seemed much less exciting and spylike, and much more cramped and dusty.

Am not feeling happy about recent developments. I'm not sure how it happened, but it seems like we are already growing into two separate people, and I don't really know how much I can trust the person she is growing into.

Although, come to think of it, I don't know if I've EVER been able to trust her. Didn't she try to kill me on our very first night together? Sure, she SAID she was only sleepwalking . . . Do I have ANY good reason to believe her?

Should I be worried about my safety, for real?

Grakking vertfarks, this isn't how I wanted things to play out.

Later

Have tried my best to persuade a cat to come console me. No dice. Have had to make do with cat-cam photos. They're a sorry substitute.

OK. Being here at home, knowing the cats have found themselves a new snuggle-buddy instead of having fun-times with me, is a bit much for me right now. Am feeling flashes of jealousy. Very unusual emotion for me. Not pleased!!!!!!!

Am heading underground.

Later

Am feeling somewhat better after a little Q.T. spent on sewer mural. Am glad in a small, vindictive way that I never told OtherMe about this place.

0100110001100001011100100
1100100111001011011000110111101
011001001010111001 LARRY LOVES
010001010101101010100100101   EM
101100011111001

Binary Larry was there, as usual. I had brushed up on my binary-to-English skills and started to translate his coding (see notes), but stopped after about 13 letters when he realized what I was doing and got embarrassed. Funneeee!

Also, he brought me flowers! AHahhahhahaAHHhahhahhaAHhaha!

Have put them in a tin can, just to be polite.

June 14

Master Pranks successfully completed, 1; disastrous family outings, 1

TERRIBLE day.

It started when Patti came up to the bedroom at sundown and woke me up. "OK, it totally makes my mind hurt, but I decided that I'm not going to run away from the facts," she said. "So where is she, my other daughter, if that's what she really is?"

Good point. "Uh . . . I don't know where she slept last night, Patti. We kind of had this fight . . . Maybe the closet?"

She wasn't in the closet, or anywhere else in the room, so Patti and I split up and searched the house for her. Actually, I spent most of that time trying to find my journal, which it turned out

I had left in the basement yesterday, and by the time I found it, ~~OtherMe~~ AnnoyingMe had turned up, and she and Patti were sitting on the couch chatting. Patti did not look mentally well at the sight of two of us, but she has agreed to deal with it if we Emilies go along on her "fun" family trip to Black Basin tonight. At least Silifordville is even closer to Black Basin than Blandindulle was, and the drive will be tolerably short.

One good thing is that we don't have to do this hiding-in-the-bedroom routine anymore. But I have not forgiven AnnoyingMe for our fight. Nor do I trust her as far as I could dropkick her!

—Anyway. We got some sandwiches packed and drove out of town to Black Basin Canyon. No matter what town we might be living in, Patti and I have been taking nighttime hikes there for years. Unfortunately, I could tell right away we were not going to have a good time. Instead of making up obnoxious lyrics to songs on the radio, the three of us sat in grim silence. Patti didn't pretend to take the wrong turns, and I didn't pretend I was late for my big cheerleading competition, or any of the other silly stuff that normally makes our road trips fun. We didn't even bother to point out our special landmarks: the phone pole that once got hit by lightning right in front of us, Old Man Dameron's Krazy Tarp Shack, and our favorite gnarly tree that looks like a cross between a skeleton and a rutabaga.

Finally (FINALLY) we arrived at the trailhead. Patti insisted on taking a cheesy family photo—we had to use the camera timer since there was no other hiker in sight.

Patti had brought special low-light flashlights for navigating in maximum darkness. And she really had picked the best night of the month for min-imum moonlight. In some small part of me, I knew she was trying to make this hike a bonding experi-ence for her and her bizarrely doubled daughter, and I could appreciate that. But in the rest of me, I felt . . . I don't know. Kind of Mad at the World, or something, and wanting the two of them to suffer for it.

But back to the Hike.

Black Basin Canyon is probably a spooky place even at noontime, but around midnight on a night with no moon, it's downright diabolical. The darkness is like tar. The birdcalls are like ghosts wailing for their dead lovers. The black, bubbling hot springs smell like the sulfurous pits of the underworld. Obviously, it's been one of my favorite spots all my life.

After so many years of hiking here, I don't even use the flashlight . . . I know all the rocks and all the trees, all the treacherous parts of the trail where you have to hug the cliff wall because there's a sheer drop of hundreds of feet on one side. I know all the places where the trail seems to end, only because it's blocked by a massive pile of boulders or trees or brush; and I know how to steer my way over or around or through every single obstacle. And as we hiked on and on, I forgot about being Mad at the World, and just enjoyed the hike.

I guess I was enjoying myself so much, it kind of slipped my mind that anyone else was with me, so I was just as surprised as Patti was when we stopped for a sandwich at our favorite lookout point, and OtherMe was gone.

Patti turned on her flashlight and swept the trail with it. No one was there.

"She's probably right behind us," I said.

Patti called for her as we walked back the way we had come, searching the sides of the trail with our flashlights. "I knew I should have brought at least one normal flashlight," she complained. "This thing is useless."

"I thought she was right with us," I said. "She's probably planning to jump out and scare the cheeks off us."

Patti gave me a terrible look. We kept searching. Patti was calling, "EMILY!" I was calling, "OTHERME!" And the next thing I knew, we were back at the trailhead, and there was no ~~OtherMe~~ AnnoyingMe in sight.

Patti was staring around wildly. I could tell she had about seven seconds of calm left before she lost it completely.

"I'm sure she's fine," I said, but Patti was already calling Search and Rescue, and I knew as I said it that she wasn't fine at all.

Top 13 thoughts running through my head as we waited at the car for Search and Rescue to arrive:

1. Excellent! AnnoyingMe has disappeared! Can we go home now?

2. Craphounds! AnnoyingMe has disappeared! I need her for our prank!

3. AnnoyingMe is clearly getting back at me for that argument we had last night.

4. If AnnoyingMe ends up needing some kind of organ or limb transplant, there is no way I'm volunteering.

5. If AnnoyingMe turns up dead, I am gonna request that her organs and limbs be frozen in case I need them in the future.

6. If helicopters have to be called in for the search, can I ride in one?

7. If Patti has to pay for the helicopters, is it going to be

taken out of my allowance?

8. I wonder what Raven's doing right now.
9. I wonder if I crossed a banana tree with a toadflax, would its fruit still be tasty?
10. Is AnnoyingMe frightened, or is she enjoying herself?
11. Does she need a sandwich as badly as I do?
12. Would it be unforgivably after-school-special if I felt the tiniest bit concerned about her? What about if I didn't?
13. How am I going to punish her for this?

Search and Rescue finally arrived. I immediately nicknamed them Jock, Biff, Tip, and Winky. Insufferable crew-cut musclebound jerks. Clearly former high school football stars who were rejected by the military, police, and fire department for being sociopathic maniacs who desperately need to feel like heroes while bullying the emotionally vulnerable families of the missing.

JOCK/BIFF/TIP/WINKY:	So, what brings you out to Black Basin in the middle of the night, ma'am?
PATTI:	I told you, we were hiking. Do you suppose we could chat later, after you've found my daughter?
J/B/T/W:	First things first . . . we need to ask a few questions to determine the best plan of attack. Now, could you

explain why you thought it would be a good idea to take your daughters on a midnight hike through one of the most treacherous areas in the state?

P: Could YOU explain how that question is going to help you find her?

J/B/T/W: No need to get huffy, ma'am. We're the experts here, not you. Now, we noticed you have a taillight out on your car . . . Were you aware that's a ticket-able offense?

I didn't wait around to hear any more, just slipped away from the car and back to the trail. No one noticed me, and soon I was out of earshot. I concentrated on making my footsteps as silent as possible and focused my attention on my ears, listening as hard as I could for anything at all. Ghostly birdcalls . . . pebbles rolling down the cliff . . . dry leaves rattling . . . I closed

my eyes for maximum concentration. Haunting birdcalls . . . grains of dirt compressing under my shoe . . . spider legs rubbing against one another . . .

Pretty soon I had reached our lookout spot.

"OtherMe!" I called, and listened.

Eerie birdcalls . . . drop of cricket spit hitting cricket wing . . . my own blood pulsing in my eardrums . . .

This was so stupid. That brat, that rotten annoying LAME piece of STINKY BRAT, she could ROT out here for all I cared. "EMILY!" I screamed. "Get out here, you stupid piece of . . . BRAT!"

Creepy birdcalls . . . moth wings beating against air molecules . . . speck of pollen falling from dried-up wildflower . . . tiny straining intake of breath through constricted throat of OtherMe, sprawled in tangle of brush on the steep hillside twenty feet above the trail.

That's where she had been lying in wait for me and Patti, planning to leap down on us, shrieking like a demon, and scare the cheeks off us; at least that's my best guess. When I found her she couldn't move or speak. She was barely breathing. Based on my knowledge of the local fauna, I was pretty sure she'd been paralyzed by a bite from a black jackal spider, which would certainly be fatal within a few minutes if I didn't do something to save her life.

Yep.

So what was I to do? Pretend I never found her? Sneak back to the car, knowing she would die before the Search and Rescue jerks got there? Or find the bite and suck the poison out the way Patti had taught me?

Let her die?

Suck the poison out?

Let her die?

Suck the poison out?

I was crouching there in the bushes, hunkered over her, tapping my chin, trying to decide what to do, when she blinked. Took a breath. Twitched her fingers. And punched me in the mouth—not very hard, what with the semiparalysis and all, but enough to get my lip bloody.

I yelled, and tackled her, and we skidded and slid twenty feet down to the trail, and started pummeling each other—by which I mean I mostly pummeled her, since she was still mostly paralyzed. But it's not like I pummeled her very hard; I just wanted to punish her a little. And I definitely did NOT mean for her to roll away from me and slide off the trail, and tumble down that slope onto those boulders, and break her leg in several places.

Of course I ran for help, and in a minute I could hear voices—Jock, Biff, Tip, and Winky were finally making their way up the trail toward us. I brought them to her as fast as I could, and if she says any different she is LYING.

So here we are, sitting in the car in the hospital parking lot, waiting for SuperAnnoyingMe to be released. Patti has been crying quite a bit. I wish she would just go wait inside, but she doesn't want to be alone, and she doesn't want the hospital staff asking questions about her identical daughters, like why they have the same name. I tried to be nice and comfort her by pointing out that if anything serious ever DID happen to one of us, at least she'd have a spare; but it just didn't seem to calm her the way I thought it would.

Later

Of course, the most annoying part about SuperAnnoyingMe getting herself semipoisoned and breaking her leg was that she couldn't help me with our prank!

Anyway, by the time we got home, Patti looked like a chunk of frozen hell on a stick and was in no shape to notice me slipping out of the house. I spent a few quality hours at Town Hall working on the Manifesto, giving it every bit of purest, darkest Strange I had, channeling all my irritations with Patti and all my anger at PatheticMe to make it as potent and raw as possible. And, you know, it might actually be a good thing PatheticMe wasn't around to see the final product, cuz this little Manifesto of mine is so Strange, it's even scaring ME.

Once everything was set, locked, and loaded, I ran the projection a few times through just to make sure it would be as mind-warping a spectacle as I had planned. And, no thanks to

PatheticMe, it IS going to be the most mind-warping thing ever to hit this town. Seriously, they better order extra straitjackets now while they still have the faculty of speech!

Later

Patti made up a bed on the living room couch for SuperAnnoyingMe. I hadn't talked to her since the whole leg-breaking, so, once Patti went to bed, I sat down on the coffee table for a little bedtime interrogation. She was heavily medicated. I had to shake her quite a bit to get any answers.

ME:	So, what was that scene in the canyon all about? Were you trying to get me separated from Patti, so you could push me off the trail? Or what?
SUPERANNOYINGME:	Not at all. I just had to . . . you know, water the bushes . . . and I got bitten. That's all.
ME:	Hm. So why punch me in the mouth when I came and found you?
SAM:	Well . . . you were just SITTING there, tapping your fingers on your chin, and obviously STRATEGIZING instead of at least TRYING to suck the poison out!
ME:	[Thinking fast.] Come on! I was just

ABOUT to suck the poison out when you punched me in the mouth! What, I'm gonna sit there and watch you DIE, as if you weren't my very own self?

And somehow right when I said it, I knew I'd said the wrong thing. Like she'd caught me in a lie. And then I realized I had no idea how she had survived a black jackal bite. Which should have been fatal within minutes. Or why she'd had the strength to punch me in the mouth. When she should have been completely paralyzed.

Something wasn't adding up, but I felt like I was on very dangerous ground with her, so I left things as they were and went to bed.

June 15
towns made Stranger, 1; reputation points gained, 0

I woke up very excited to check out the newly strange Silifordville. Patti and AnnoyingMe were still asleep when I got up, so I fixed dinner for myself and hurried out of the house. I snuck around town a bit, which was easier than usual, since there was zero traffic on the roads. And no pedestrians anywhere. Definitely ominous, but not quite what I was hoping for. I got bored after a while and went out to the skate park for some practice. That place was empty too, which suited me fine, at least for a couple of hours, when this kid showed up by himself, looking . . . I don't know, sketched out of his mind somehow.

He ran to me and started in:

KID:	You seen Froggy?
ME:	No.
K:	Killer?
ME:	No.
K:	What about PooDog?
ME:	No.
K:	Dirtbike?
ME:	No.
K:	Mushroom?
ME:	No.
K:	Junebug?
ME:	No.
K:	Biscuit?
ME:	No.
K:	[Hyperventilating.] Crap, I gotta find them . . .

And he skated away. I gave him a minute, then skated covertly after him and spied as he searched the town for his friends. He rang a few doorbells, then ran in and out of the library, then snuck under the fence of the high school, and then finally skated over to Town Hall, where a quick peek in the windows of the main auditorium told me where most of the townspeople have been all evening: frozen in their seats as the Manifesto of Strange plays out in their heads.

EXCELLENT!

I'm gonna check this out further, gotta go—

Later

Wonderful, marvelous, hilarious Strangeness is taking place at Town Hall! As soon as the kid saw his friends through the windows, he ran around to the front and into the auditorium. I waited outside for a few minutes, but he never came back out, so I peeked through the windows again and spotted him in a small crowd of people standing near the back of the room.

They all looked the same—just standing straight, looking forward, no expressions, hands at their sides . . . it was so weird. And the Manifesto was still playing—so every few minutes, some new sucker from outside would go in to see what was wrong and just freeze in their tracks, staring forward, expressionless.

GOOD STUFF!

Later

Someone finally figured out NOT to go into the auditorium, and called the police instead. Several of the dimmer officers have rushed in and been frozen, nevertheless. Ahhahhhahhhahhaah! But now quite a few of them are milling about outside Town Hall, calling for reinforcements and advice. I am hiding in the bushes, enjoying the confusion and waiting to see how it all plays out.

Later

They have (finally) managed to turn off the Manifesto. Of all people, it was our crazy neighbor Venus Fang Fang who accomplished it. I give her credit for figuring it out, since OtherMe and I took precautions to ensure it would play as long as we wanted it to. Now let's just hope she is not capable of tracing this back to us!

Anyway, now that the hypnotic power of my Manifesto has released their little minds, the townspeople have fled Town Hall decidedly stranger than they were yesterday. I'm seeing a big increase in non sequiturs being screamed at volume eleven, inappropriate (and unwelcome) nudity, the eating of grass and dirt, what-have-you. On the downside, there are lots of police out on the prowl, herding loonies into paddy wagons. (I stayed safely under cover, just in case. You never know what a police officer may consider loony.) News vans everywhere. Cameramen are doing their best to shoot footage of weirdos. I caught a few seconds of the mayor being interviewed on the steps of Town Hall, but that was cut short when she started screaming out the names of random fruits and vegetables.

SUCCESS!

Um . . . only one drawback, which is that the reaction around town is so incredibly, closed-mindedly negative, I am not going to be able to take credit.

Hmm. I may need to go home and sabotage our TV reception so that Patti and AnnoyingMe do not see the news.

Hmmm. If AnnoyingMe finds out what is going on in town, I will try to make her think it is all her fault.

Hmmmm. I wonder. If she finds out what I did, is she likely to turn me in?

I may need to preemptively destroy her!

June 16

disturbing medication dreams forgotten, 23; journals compromised, 1

BIG TROUBLE!!!!

I DID NOT WRITE THE LAST TWO DAYS OF JOURNAL ENTRIES!!!!!!

Just woke up from harrowing medication-muddled dreams, decided to write them down if I could, and grabbed my journal off the coffee table. Am so heavily medicated, I could not remember anything I had written since my accident, so I flipped back a few pages to catch up with myself. That's when I discovered that OtherMe and I apparently switched journals two days ago, and then switched them back again today. No idea how this could have happened, but in my current foggy state, I can easily imagine Mom moving us to a new town without me realizing it.

Am now desperately trying to A) remember what I wrote about in the past two days and whether it was incriminating, and B) decide whether I think OtherMe knows about the switch. If she does, she will know that I know that she plans to destroy me! Must come up with plan for

June 17

signatures on cast, 1; decisions made to flush medication down toilet, 5; doses of medication gladly taken, 5; cat attention units, 0; personal slaves acquired, 1; plans for neutralizing OtherMe before she neutralizes me, 0

Was not able to write much at all yesterday due to awful brain-fuzzing medication. Will flush all pills down the toilet as soon I can work up the personal courage to take the pain.

Maybe later. My leg hurts like . . . OK, am too fuzzed to come up with juicy simile at the moment, but be assured that it hurts really, REALLY bad. Leave it to me to break a leg in the most complicated way possible. Am looking at bed rest for semiforever and crutches for approximately eternity, or at least the rest of the summer.

In other news, I have noticed cat-tooth imprints on my journal. Am now thinking the cats are probably responsible for getting our journals mixed up. Am glad they just dragged my journal around the house, rather than defiling it. Would not be able to fall asleep facedown in it anymore, that's for sure.

Later

Am dying of worry, pain, withdrawal from cat affection, and fear for my life. Am in terrible mental haze due to evil medication. Keep falling asleep and dreaming that I am one of the loonies created by the Manifesto. I sure feel like one. Am suffering terrible guilt over having participated in that disaster. It's not what I wanted to happen!!!!! I thought everyone was going to have a nice, mind-blowing, life-altering experience, then go out and . . . you know, paint sewer murals, or . . . make raven-golems . . . I don't know . . . and, instead, it looks like we have just brutalized them with our own Strangeness and semidestroyed their minds in the process.

GAH. Clearly, it was a big mistake to want other people to be Strange. I mean, even if it had worked exactly as I imagined, how lame would THAT be? Everyone fighting for space in the sewer to paint their mural? Or creating preternatural beings out of miscellaneous animal parts? Raven is trouble enough. Imagine all the havoc that HUNDREDS of Ravens would cause. [Shudder.]

It's not like I have this burning need to be different from other people, but I also don't have any desire for them to be like me. Wish I had never gone along with this plan in the first place!

Later

OK, WHERE ARE THE CATS? I am in insane withdrawal. I need to pet a cat NOW. I need to stare into Mystery's infinite eyes and hear Sabbath's retarded meows of love. I need to feel NeeChee's whiskers rubbed against my skin. I need Miles' claws to make bread on my stomach. GIVE ME KITTYCAT TIME!

Am so doped up on pain meds, I can't even tell if Retarded Meows of Love would be a good band name or not. FOR SUCK!!!!!!!!!!!!!

Later

Just woke up in horrible anxiety. I desperately need to come up with an excellent plan for neutralizing OtherMe before she neutralizes me. Am afraid I will talk in my sleep, and betray that I've read her journal entries, and she will decide to accelerate her plans to destroy me.

My thoughts are very confused right now, but here are the top things moiling in my mind:

1. OtherMe and I are DIFFERENT.
2. She has lied to me, broken promises to Mom, considered letting me die of spider bite, pummeled me, warped our inspiring Manifesto into something that has psychically damaged hundreds of people, and, oh yeah, threatened to preemptively destroy me.
3. I don't know why I didn't really think of this before now, but OBVIOUSLY, one of us must be the original Emily, and the other one must be a copy.
4. I feel like I'm the original. Though I assume OtherMe probably feels the same. Based on the fact that she is considering getting rid of me.
5. There must be a way to tell the original from the copy.
6. Unfortunately, I don't know what that might be. Neither one of us looks blurry around the edges. Though that IS how I feel right now, thanks to pain meds.
7. Am very vulnerable right now. Mom signed my cast and I slept right through it. Stupid medication!!! Will try self-hypnosis for the pain instead. Cannot afford to let my guard down at a time like this.
8. I realize this is whiny, but I need to whine a little about how wrong it is that the cats have abandoned me NOW, of all times. Before OtherMe was on the scene, if I even

had so much as a painful hangnail, all four cats would be crawling on me, purring and giving cat sympathy.

9. Am noticing unusually high whininess factor. Is this a sign that I am the fake one?

10. Mother of Pearl! Have just realized that my recent lack of cat attention is clearly a result of the duplication. What am I, slow? At least they are avoiding OtherMe as well and not just reacting to me being the fake one.

11. I had better not be the fake one!!!!!!!!!!!! Am suffering serious identity crisis here!!!!!!!!!!!!!!!!!!!

12. Just had another one of my lame crying fits. Man, I NEVER used to break down like this before the duplication. Maybe this is more evidence that I am the fake one.

13. If ~~OtherMe~~ EvilMe IS the real one, then I am going to have to revise my general opinion of Emily Strange.

Later

It occurred to me to check those tapeworms I duplicated to see if I can tell the original from the duplicate. Mom has been a very good sport and fetched them from Experiment Corner in my bedroom. But unfortunately they look exactly the same to me.

Have given up on scientific inquiry for the moment, and asked the Magic 8 Ball which of us is the real one. Response was "BETTER NOT TELL YOU NOW." Probably because I am the fake one.

OK, am putting away the Magic 8 Ball. I really need to return to scientific inquiry and come up with a trustworthy way to tell the real Me from the fake Me!

Later

Mom has just been in to check on me. Conversation went something like this:

MOM: So, are you accepting or refusing your meds this hour?

ME: Accepting! Accepting!

M: Good. The pain's been making you awfully cranky.

ME: No kidding. Hypnosis, my cheeks! I'll try it next time I have a hangnail.

M: Hey, did you just crack a joke? That's progress.

ME: Thanks. I've been getting pretty bored with my own whininess. Hey, could you do me a favor and bring me a cat? Any cat?

M: No problem.

ME: Also, I was thinking it would raise my spirits if we organized some kind of fun family-oriented game. Something along the lines of "This Is Your Life" Jeopardy?

M: . . . Sure . . . but . . .

ME: You think the other Emily and I will be perfectly

matched, huh? Well, let's just say I'm investigating that hypothesis.

Mom is game and has agreed to be the moderator. However, she pointed out that each of us really should write half the questions. I guess she's right. I mean, if I AM the fake one, I need to know!

Later

Mom has just been in to give me Sabbath. He hissed at me and I held him and petted him until I felt bad for keeping him prisoner, and then he launched himself off my cast, trying madly to get away, and it hurt like a FLUTTERPLACKING PIGBARK.

Things MUST improve tomorrow!

June 18

signatures on cast, 2; cat attention units, 0; FakeCats created, 1; Jeopardy questions written, 97; Jeopardy questions approved by Mom, 66; whininess factor, 11; plans to eliminate EvilMe, 0

Day Four on the couch. Since cats will not come near me, I asked Mom to bring me some of the lovely insane stuffed animals I have creatively stitched up over the years. Raided them for body parts and cobbled together a plushy black stuffed cat. It doesn't purr or snuggle, but it also doesn't hiss or flee, so I'm clutching it to my heart for all I'm worth.

Now craft hour is over, and I am currently dying of boredom rather than fear, guilt, and pain. Would like to say it's an improvement, but it's not. Tried books and video games, but brain is too fuzzy from medication for those. Tried TV, but EvilMe has sabotaged it. That's OK, I know it's too disgustingly stupid even for a brain as fuzzed-out as mine is right now. And watching the news would only drive me into Shame Spiral, Part IV.

When not on the phone to the cable company, complaining that their repairmen have not fixed our reception, Mom is moping around the house. Am not sure, in my zoned-out mental state, whether she knows about the Manifesto and the havoc it has caused. Am not looking forward to the inevitable meltdown over that. Will keep fingers crossed.

On the brighter side, Mom is forcing EvilMe to be my personal slave since I am totally immobile. I do not think EvilMe knows we switched journals. Aside from practical exchanges like "Here's your sandwich" and "Bring me the bedpan," we have not really been speaking. I mean, we haven't been planning any more jolly episodes of cooperative prankery, that's for sure. If/when we do have a real conversation again, I'm not sure what I will say to her. What is there to say? Thanks for finding me in the canyon, and for not sucking the poison out? Thanks for knocking me off the trail and breaking my leg? Oh, and thanks for appearing out of NOWHERE, turning my cats against me, causing mental anguish for Mom, and basically ruining what was supposed to be a fun, exploration-and-experiment-filled summer of SOLITUDE! What am I going to accomplish with a big old broken leg? A crossword puzzle? Maybe I'll crochet a potholder? GAHHH!!!!

Pain is making me crabby again. Need more medication. Will ring my personal slave.

Personal slave not responding to her summons. Go figure. ~~Will make Mom punish her.~~ What am I saying? Will need to punish her myself, clearly. Must quit complaining and take action. Will need to build some kind of elevator so I can get upstairs to my bedroom, and rig up an elaborate pulley system in the room so I can work on experiments and monitor cat activity from my bed.

Later

Have crocheted potholder. Used yarn I braided from my own hair. Had been saving up hair for years and had a large box of it that really needed to be put to good use. Mom thanked me for the potholder and tried to seem enthusiastic, but I could tell she was imagining the smell of burning hair, and wondering where she could hide the hideous thing. Will have to think of non-kitchen-related uses for the rest of the hair.

Later

Just realized that EvilMe signed my cast while I was asleep. Am very annoyed that she signed it "Emily." Am also somewhat terrified that she was able to do so without waking me up. Nothing I can do about it.

Gave Mom a batch of questions for our Jeopardy showdown. Here are some prime ones:

1. I used <u>this disease</u> as a clever excuse to get out of attending the first through third grades.
2. I successfully faked <u>this supernatural skill</u> for an audience of skeptics when I was 9.
3. My patent on <u>this creative use of ordinary dirt</u> has pretty much paid the rent for the past 3 years.
4. I found the abandoned kitten we now know as Miles under a Dumpster in <u>this humorously named small town</u>.
5. <u>This officer of the law</u> was the first (and last) to succeed in handcuffing me—if only for a moment.

6. A sugar-cube diorama of <u>this famous natural disaster</u> landed me in psychiatric evaluation for a year.
7. I used a spirited game of Calamity Poker and an artificial sandstorm to cleverly distract <u>this would-be Romeo</u> from going on a date with Raven.
8. Over the years, a shrine I constructed to <u>this Surrealist painter</u> has caused the faintings of 3 housekeepers, 7 neighbors, and 1 social worker.
9. Mystery joined our household when Patti rescued her from <u>this potentially deadly scenario.</u>
10. I used my Magic 8 Ball to successfully advise <u>this leader of state</u> through a minor national crisis.
11. Before I rescued him from a recently deceased cat lady's pestilential home, Sabbath was named after <u>this iconic science-fiction villain.</u>
12. NeeChee's striped tail is the result of an unfortunate run-in with <u>these 4 common household chemicals.</u>
13. The month I spent at a summer camp run by <u>this celebrity</u> was cut short by an unfortunate incident involving a feather boa, a video camera, and 20 gallons of rubber cement.

Mom has compiled my questions with EvilMe's and eliminated the duplicates. Huh. Yeah. Eliminated the duplicates. Wish I could do more of that, myself.

Later

Just woke up and the box of hair is gone. No more hair projects for today. It's OK. Am very sleepy.

Later

Have just had a horrifying nightmare in which ~~EvilMe~~ EvilOne used my hair to bring down evil voodoo on me, causing my leg to come out of the cast with the foot pointing backward. Should have had better security for that box of hair!

Ugh. Am clearly not making smart decisions. Am not enjoying horrifying nightmares like I normally would. Am not spontaneously coming up with delightful revenge ideas. Am not able to write dozens of fiendishly difficult Jeopardy questions that will win me the game. Way too many of my fiendishly difficult questions have been duplicates of questions EvilOne has already written.

Later

EvilOne has just been in to see me. Our conversation went a little something like this:

EVILONE:	Yeah, so, what's the point of this Jeopardy game, anyway?
ME:	Uhhhhh . . . idle entertainment . . . ?
EO:	Yeah, right. You're trying to prove that you

know more about being Emily Strange
than I do. You think I'm a just a copy of
you, right? A FakeYou?

ME: Oh. Well. Huh. Ummmm . . .

EO: [Sighing. Rolling eyes. Thumping me
casually on the cast.] Whatever. As long
as you understand that you're going to lose, and
I'm going to punish you for losing.

ME: [Pretending the thumping does not hurt like a
flutterplacking pigbark.] What if I win?

EO: Then I'll punish you for winning. But you won't
win, cuz you're a silly little FakeMe.

GULP! Am now wondering what I think she meant by "punish."
Not to mention her entry of June 15, and what she meant by "preemptively destroy"—I mean, would she actually kill me? Could I
actually kill her? Am hoping it does not come to that, but am flat
out of ideas on how to resolve my doppelgänger dilemma.

Have wished her away many times, but she keeps showing up
again.

Very frustrating.

Later

Am trying to stay positive by focusing on how much better life
will be when I'm off the couch. Among other things, I really

would like to get out of the house to do some spying on Venus Fang Fang. It astonishes me that she would be able to shut down our Manifesto. I mean, there can't be more than a dozen people in the world who know what a Vanian-Jugg circuit is, let alone how to disable it. Am very impressed! Not to mention afeard. Fingers crossed she can't trace it back to us!!!!!

June 19

tar units used, 3; past successes revisited, 133; Jeopardy questions written, 47; Jeopardy questions approved by Mom, 7

Life has improved slightly. Am back to using self-hypnosis for leg pain. Was about to flush medication down the toilet when I reflected that I may be able to secretly dose EvilOne's food with it at some point in the future. That cheered me quite a bit. Am up and around on crutches now despite the crunching pain. Totally against doctor's orders. Have painted my cast with liquid black rock to hide signatures. Should probably have used regular black paint but was hit by small flash of inspiration/blind hope that the black rock might also help with the pain. Not really sure it is working, but at least I'm mobile.

Also, my cast looks a lot cooler.

Later

Am in a MUCH better mood than yesterday! Am now reviewing old family photo albums and scrapbooks to gear up for the big Jeopardy challenge, which is scheduled for two days from now. Our family photo albums and scrapbooks are AMAZING! I feel sorry for people who do not have photos of themselves training cats to stand on one another in pyramid formation, or synthesizing amino acids in home laboratory, or completing giant homemade paint-by-numbers replicas of Bosch paintings, or reanimating lifeless human flesh and miscellaneous bird organs into a working golem. (See some favorites on next page.)

Speaking of golems . . . Hmm.

Five minutes later

OK. Have just reread entries of June 7 to June 9. WHY, WHY, WHY didn't I realize back then that EvilOne was not sleepwalking at all, but actually trying to kill me? And that Raven was in fact rescuing me, not threatening my life? And that EvilOne OBVIOUSLY got rid of Raven to make destroying me easier?

I can't believe she actually had me believing that I was commanding Raven to kill, or that I had subconscious hostility toward Mom or Mystery. I mean, MOM and MYSTERY! My two favorite living beings in the world!

Must get Raven back, and fast!!!!

Thirty seconds later

Oh no. What if Raven was at the ribbon-cutting ceremony and has been turned into a gibbering loony? I mean . . . more of a gibbering loony.

Am waking Mom up right now.

Later

Just had a little straight talk with Mom. This is what I found out:

1. First off, we are blattering LUCKY that MOM didn't go to the stupid ribbon-cutting ceremony!

2. She says it has been practically impossible to buy groceries, catch a bus, or get a TV repairman out to the house.

3. Looting and vandalism are way up, and the police are too busy rounding up loonies to do much about it.

4. Mom has already taken it upon herself to check up on Raven. Let us be mightily thankful that on the evening of the ribbon-cutting ceremony, Raven was safe at home with Bebe, who was feeling poorly.

5. Gigi, however, is another story. Mom located her in a dark corner of the psych ward, where she was finger-painting with . . . well, something no one should finger-paint with, and singing mellow love songs from the 1970s. Mom says the image will be burned into her mind for all eternity.

6. Mom hates to think what might have happened if
   Raven had attended the ribbon-cutting ceremony: My
   superstrong golem would probably be running amok,
   battling loonies and police alike. (At least, Mom SAYS
   she hates to think of it, but clearly she ENJOYS thinking
   about it.)
7. Mom doesn't have any evidence, or at least no evidence
   that would stand up in court . . . but for all intents and
   purposes, she knows we did this.
8. The incident has made the national news, and a major
   investigation is under way, so she is assuming and hoping
   that we covered our tracks.
9. She is assuming and hoping that we did not actually
   intend to psychically damage most of the townspeople.
10. She is assuming and hoping that we are already hard at
    work on a solution that will reverse the aforementioned
    psychic damage. (I did not have the heart to contradict
    her. No need to crush her spirit just yet.)
11. She also has her hopes that we are working on a solution to
    this whole duplication thing.
12. She admits that coming up with a solution to the
    whole duplication thing might be kinda taxing to the
    imagination, especially if one were suffering with pain
    and medication.
13. She is tired, very tired, of all the trouble we've had in our

19 days in Silifordville, but would like to think that we can get through it and last out the year, at least.

I let Mom go back to bed and am lying here on the couch making some plans. As soon as morning comes, I will call Bebe and see if I can persuade her to return Raven.

Later—broad daylight

Phoned Bebe and asked her to return Raven to me as soon as possible, but the conversation did not go well.

ME: Bebe, I'm telling you, it's a matter of life and death!

BEBE: Well, same here. Gigi's gone gaga and so has our maid, and who's going to do all this dusting?

ME: You need a state-of-the-art golem to do your DUSTING?

B: Golem?

ME: Gahhhh! I need Raven to come be my BODYGUARD!

B: I don't think that will work very well. She's not even doing the dusting.

ME: GAHHH— Wait, she's not doing what you tell her to do?

B: No, she just sits there with her mouth open,

and it's really creepy.

ME: Did you try saying "Emily" before you told her to do the dusting?

B: Yes, I tried "Emily," "jockstrap," "poopcake," "barf-bag," "Titicaca," "codpiece," "Mulva," "Dolores," "dissemination," and "kumquat," but she just sits there.

ME: [Not laughing. Not laughing at all.] This is serious. I'll be there in ten minutes.

Later

Bad stuff! Really bad stuff!

Got to Bebe's house (which DOES need a good dusting—if by "dusting" you mean "adding several centuries' worth of dust") to find Raven sitting around with her mouth open, as described. She is not looking good at all. I guess I really should have paid more attention to the pedicure scene I witnessed on her first night here, and made some extrapolations from that. Anyhow, the results are terrifying. They have bought her a new wig, which, admittedly, is a lot less ratty than her old wig, which had been partially burned and then torn apart for use in vehicle repairs, but at least had CHARACTER and HISTORY. Her clothing is also new and, unlike her old clothing, is totally lacking in rips, stains, safety pins, staples, handmade patches, handsewn instructions for returning Raven to her home, and drawings of vampire-cat-zombie-ninja-monkey-mutants. Someone has obviously spent some time choosing tasteful accessories to coordinate with her outfit, including a silk scarf to hide the Frankenstein-monster stitches I spent all that time tattooing on her neck, which I thought were not only hilarious and tuff-looking, but a nice literary reference. She's wearing quite a bit of expertly applied makeup. And she's apparently been to a tanning salon. Ugh!!! To sum it up, Raven is looking a lot less like a well-used, well-loved, grungy old golem, and a lot more like a well-heeled, well-groomed, attractive NORMAL WOMAN.

I didn't really know where to start, so I tried a little small talk.

ME:	Man, Raven, I haven't seen you in so long. I mean, how long has it been ... [counting days]
RAVEN:	Thirteen hours.
ME:	... You saw me thirteen hours ago?

R: Uh-huh.

ME: Right. And what did "we" do?

R: Looted stores. Mostly.

ME: [Gasping to myself at the EVIL
        of the OtherMe!!!!]. Raven, could you please stand
        on one foot and bark like a dog?

R: . . .

ME: EMILY. Stand on one leg!

R: . . .

ME: [Screaming. Making Bebe whimper in fear.]
        EMILY, I say! EMILY! Bark like a dog!

R: . . .

ME: WHAT HAS SHE DONE TO YOU??????????????

Later

Have spent the past four hours in Bebe's living room, taking
Raven apart and putting her back together.

After much investigation, I finally found a line of code buried in her programming that I didn't recognize. It prevents her
from obeying commands from anyone but "13-34-567/45-32-741/
9-55-4/88-123-42/97-16-197." It's a simple code for "Emily." —Well,
it's simple if you know the code, and which edition of <u>Occult
Thermodynamics and You</u> to use to crack it.

What I haven't been able to figure out is why this code allows
EvilOne's commands to work and not mine.

I mean . . . Aren't I Emily too?

Worrisome!!!!!!!

Anyway, for now, I fixed it by changing "Emily" to "Emily and Emily." For some reason, this works. Very . . . strange.

Later—back at home

I got Bebe to drive me and Raven home. Have explained to Mom that Raven needed to be back for just a little while for reprogramming. Mom seemed fine with that.

I can only hope that EvilOne does not look into Raven's coding, or she will know I have control of Raven again.

OK. Raven has been stationed in the armchair next to the couch. Am feeling slightly safer. Going to sleep.

June 20

booby traps remodeled, 0; cat attention units, ½; Jeopardy questions written, 23; Jeopardy questions accepted by Mom, 2; legs feeling semihealed, 1

My leg is feeling MUCH better. Have taken no medication today. Mind is also improving. I give all credit to the liquid black rock.

Have kept Raven constantly by my side, but even so, I've been feeling the strong need for self-preservation. Have visited my various hidey-holes around the house, only to find that ALL of them have brand-new booby traps!!!! Oh, the unspeakable evil!

Attempted to neutralize and revise them in very subtle ways so that the changes were impossible to detect, BUT, I cannot say I've been successful. In fact, I was mostly only successful in flinging myself to the floor just in time to avoid sprays of icy water, catapults of gravel, etc. Hopefully my failure is just a result of lingering leg pain. Cannot blame the medication anymore. Cannot believe the EvilOne has been so busy. I suppose this is the beginning of her plan to destroy me.

Later

I waited until EvilOne left the house, then lurched upstairs to the bedroom, only to be scared out of my wits and semideafened by a barrage of extremely loud firecrackers. Jarbing frambax! I LIKED those eardrums.

Later

Have not been able to come up with reciprocal booby trap on bedroom door. Am becoming soft. Have settled for whipping up a fast-acting, odorless bleaching agent and adding it to shampoo. Am looking forward to hearing EvilOne's shriek when she sees herself in the mirror after her next shower. Am extremely cheered. It's amazing what a little proactive revenge work can do for a girl's self-esteem. Should write a self-help book on the Power of Positive Revenge. My 13-point PPR course would train people to quit whining like a pack of babies and start taking control of their lives (and the lives of their enemies) through creative prankery and fun, diabolical psychological torture. I WOULD write it, too, if I cared the least little bit about people's self-esteem, or if I didn't think I would immediately have the cheeks sued off me by spoilsports.

June 21
satisfying pranks inflicted, 1; self-esteem points regained, 13

Woke up at nightfall, tied to the couch. Raven was nowhere around. Had to work long and hard to get untied. Uncool!! But not unexpected. I'd stashed some miscellaneous tools in my pockets before going to sleep, just in case. If EvilOne hadn't tied my arms down so tightly, I'd have been free in way less time. Anyway, it could have been worse. At least it gave me an excuse not to take the first shower. Midway through my knot-work, I heard the much-anticipated screams from EvilOne when she saw her hair. It gave me the courage I needed to go on.

Later

Have found Raven locked in the birdcage. Luckily she has not been reprogrammed. YET.

Later

Am in the middle of dinner with Mom and EvilOne, who arrived at the table sporting pale blond hair with hideous yellow streaks!

AH HAHAHAH AH HAHA! She has had to endure Mom's comments of "Wow, E! Your hair looks so . . . cute?" I have added lots of friendly remarks like "You're all set for cheerleading tryouts!" and "I hear blands have more fun! Oh, sorry . . . did I say BLANDS? AHA HAH HA HAH AHA HA HAHAHA!!" I've been watching her closely to see if there will be tears, but she is a tough character.

Man, this feels good. Reckon I will suffer for it, but it's soooooooooo worth it.

OK, Mom has just asked me for the third time to wrap it up with my journal and eat my dinner before it is stone-cold. Hard to resist writing triumphant entries about EvilOne right in front of her while she stabs evil death glares at me, but I AM kinda hungry.

Later

There is no way I am the fake one!!!!

Out of the blue, Mom has given me just that little bit of an edge I needed to win the game. The three of us were finishing dinner. Our conversation went a little bit like this:

MOM: I was thinking you should maybe ask Great-Aunt Millie about, ahem, you know, your duplication . . . experiment . . . thingy?

EVILONE: Who, now?

ME: [Staring at her.] Um, Great-Aunt MILLIE? Transparent lady, lives in the attic?

EO: What? Someone else lives here? Here in this house?

M: [Giving her a Look.] Are you trying to be funny? Show respect for your spirit elders.

EO: [Clueless. But playing it cool.] I've got NOTHING if I don't have respect for my spirit elders.

ME: [Annoyed.] Dude, Patti . . . you know Great-Aunt Millie likes to be called a poltergeist. [To EvilOne.] So, what, did you take a blow to the head recently, or do you really not know about our poltergeist?

EO: [Trying out a look of contempt.] Great-Aunt Millie? Of COURSE I know about her.

ME: So then you know about . . . the curse.

EO: Yeah. [Long pause. Seriously long pause.] Yep.

ME: [Laughing cheeks off. Formulating a whole bunch of last-minute Jeopardy questions involving Great-Aunt Millie.]

M: E, please, no making fun of your doppelgänger at the table, huh?

Later

GOOD STUFF!!!!! My leg was feeling entirely pain free, so I carefully and secretly sawed off the cast to investigate. It appears to be completely back to normal. I can only assume that liquid black rock heals broken bones!!!

—Also, I have put the cast back on and camouflaged the sawblade marks. No need to let EvilOne know I am not still crippled!

—Also, note to self: If I ever have to wear a cast again, should refrain from shoving bits of Mom's potpourri down it with a coat hanger, no matter how stinky it gets. It's not worth it!!!!!

Later

EvilOne lost no time coloring her hair back to black. To look at her, you would never know the whole blonding incident happened. But I'm sure she won't let this go unavenged.

Later

Mom has not rejected any of the last-minute Great-Aunt Millie questions. We now have an entire category devoted to her. There is no way I can lose!!!!!

One long Jeopardy game later

I have lost, 2,390 to 3,310!

Cannot even believe I am writing this, but clearly EvilOne knows more about ~~my our her~~ Emily's life than I do!

As EvilOne jubilantly scored her final points, loudly proclaimed herself the winner, and did an obnoxious victory dance around the living room, I could see by Mom's expression that she was coming to some uncomfortable realizations: A) EvilOne and I were NOT perfectly matched after all; B) we were clearly taking this game more seriously than she expected; and C) there would likely be Some Tension in the household now that a winner had been declared.

Mom semidiscreetly crumpled up the construction paper crowns she had probably expected to give us after a tied game, and tried to make me feel better by blaming the pain/self-hypnosis/medication. But the truth is that EVILONE WON. Evil one. Evil won. Unbelievable.

I really thought I was onto something big when I discovered, the night of our canyon hike, that EvilOne didn't have all the same memories I have. And in hindsight, it's not that it was a bad idea to use this against her in a game of "This Is Your Life" Jeopardy. It's just that, as it turns out, she is more of an expert than I am on being me.

I did at least prove to her, to Mom, and to myself that EvilOne has no knowledge of the following important events in the Life of Emily Strange:

1. That time when Great-Aunt Millie got herself trapped in the water pipes, and all the faucets screamed when anyone turned them on.

2. That time she lost some psychic weight, or something, and kept sinking through the floors. She would even sink right through you if you didn't keep a lookout. And how we had to get a ghostbuster to paint the attic floor with this special paint that ghosts can't go through. And how we had to lie to him about there being an actual ghost in the house or he'd try to exterminate her. Yeah, that was awesome.

3. Names of 3 of the towns Mom and I have lived in.

4. Names of 7 alternative tunings I've invented for the electric guitar.

5. Names of ANY of the 77 inventions I have patented.

6. Name of Zenith's cat back in Blandindulle. And that was only last month!!!

7. Name of the shifty thief back in Yaktown who taught me the basics of lock-picking.

8. Name of the lock-picking maneuver I used to break into said shifty thief's home and steal back Mom's pearl necklace.

9. The stories behind how I got each of my cats.

10. What I used in the duplicator to finally get it working.

11. Names of 7 of our 12 (known) dead great-aunts.

12. How I managed to animate a few dead bird parts to make Raven.

13. How I collected a bunch of black jackal spiders, milked

their venom, and administered it to myself, slowly over time, in order to build up an immunity.

Unfortunately, EvilOne has proven that I do not recall the following:

1. The name I gave the skateboard trick I used to win last year's Teen Shred Invitational.
2. The name of pretty much any skateboard trick ever made up by anyone.
3. The atomic weight of yttrium. Nor its oxidation state.
4. How to use an interferometer for basic plasma diagnostics.
5. The formula for calculating terminal velocity.
6. The story behind the phrase "nothing but a thin broth" and why it makes Patti and EvilOne laugh so hard.
7. What the so-called "dark code" is or what it does.
8. The name of the merry prankster who taught me the basics of booby-trapping.
9. The type of booby trap I used to prove my tactical superiority to said prankster.
10. How to use an X-10 switch to turn lights on and off . . . in other people's homes.
11. Names of 5 common household items that can be used as explosives.

12. Names of 4 of the towns Mom and I have lived in.
13. Exactly why it is we move so often. (They still haven't told me. Am not happy.)

Later

As I should have expected, losing that Jeopardy game is having more consequences than just lower self-esteem. EvilOne is being an insufferable troll about the whole thing. She is referring to me as "the fake one," kicking me in the cast whenever possible, and sitting around staring at me, tapping her chin in an unsettling way, as if lost in thought as to the best way to destroy me.

Man. I want SO MUCH to be the Real Emily, but the evidence isn't pointing to it. On the other hand, surely the Real Emily would know about Great-Aunt Millie??? Not to mention all the other stuff I know that EvilOne doesn't. Obviously, we are not Velveteen Rabbits, and the issue is a little more complex than just Real vs. Fake.

I wish I could tell what is going on in EvilOne's head right now, especially her thoughts re: destroying me. I mean, I was drugged, immobile, and Ravenless for several days, yet there were no murder attempts. I wonder what has changed. Has she decided there might be some value to keeping me around? I know it's not in me to kill EvilOne. Our skateboarding skills (just to touch on the tip of things) would be lost forever. Am ~~assuming~~ hoping she feels the same on her side. May need to play the guitar more often while she's around, just to remind her of my virtuo-spasticality.

Later—2:00 a.m.

I am going to sneak out of the house and work on my sewer mural. Have missed the outdoors, the sewers, and art-style self-therapy quite a bit. I could use a little boost in my opinion of myself right about now. Hope all is well down there. Oh clapjacks, hope Binary Larry did not get his mind scrambled too badly by the Manifesto! That kid was already fairly loony.

Must remember to be extra watchful for booby traps when I get back.

Later

Took the bus out to the sewer, pulled off that nasty cast, and painted, painted, painted until the lovely crazy swirly dreamy splendor took my mind off the failed Jeopardy game, my possible fakeness, and the evil of the EvilOne.

Binary Larry was there, which surprised me, since it was way past his bedtime. And he WAS a little more loony than normal, but mostly it seemed like he had just woken up. That, and he was maybe more impressed with my mural than he had a right to be.

Our conversation went a little something like this:

BINARY LARRY: Oh, man, wow, I mean, yeah, so groggin.

ME: Hmm.

BL: Yeah, I'm serious, it reminds me of that crazy thing they showed at Town Hall.

ME: Wha—what are you talking about?

BL: You don't know? The ribbon-cutting ceremony? Those flyers? The free candy?

ME: Oh, right. Uh, did you go?

BL: Ghuhff! You think I'd be standing around talking to you if I went?

ME: That bad, huh?

BL: Oh yeah, man, I mean, all my friends are in the psych ward now. PooDog, Dirtbike, Mushroom, Treehole, Biscuit . . . but my mom was making me do yard work at the time, so, yeah.

ME: So, why do you say my painting reminds you of it?

BL: Oh, I don't know, I guess it's because it looks just like those clips they're showing on TV all the time now.

ME: WHAT? Why are they doing that?

BL: Oh . . . you know . . .

ME: WHAT????? Spill it, you.

BL: You KNOW . . . that whole . . . thing.

GAHHHH!!!! Binary Larry is not QUITE as difficult

dReam house

162

to talk to as Raven, but he's blipping close! It would drive me straight bonkers to record our entire conversation, but safe to say, I grilled him for a while, then released him when it was obvious he was too sleep-deprived to stay on topic. I got the following sinister facts and town gossip out of him:

1. There is indeed a major investigation of the Manifesto under way, and every townsperson suspected of the slightest artistic inclination has been hauled into the police station and thoroughly harassed.

2. Since no one has the smallest scrap of information, everyone has been giving the police the names of other artistic folks in exchange for their freedom.

3. Binary Larry was ratted out by his own art teacher. He was at the station for 5 hours before his mom pitched enough of a fit to get him released.

4. I am YARBING lucky that BL has a sweet spot for me and did not breathe a word about me to the police. (So he swears, anyway.)

5. Am also very lucky that no other living soul knows about my incriminating sewer mural.

6. So many of the Silifordville townspeople have gone stark guano crazy that food supplies are running low, stores are going out of business, and basic services (like water and power) are in danger of being cut off. Don't I watch the news?

7. The police are taxed to their limits what with loony control and artist interrogation, so everyone who still has their wits about them is doing their best to take advantage of the situation.

8. For example, burglaries have jumped 567%.

9. And vandalism, up 789%.

10. And looting . . . well, there's been 7 cases. Up from 0.

11. And criminals from neighboring towns have started moving in. In fact, 2 rival gangs from nearby Centerville (the Ratts and the 12th Street Toughs—man, they could use some coaching on those names) have scheduled a contest to see how many cars they can put out of commission by knifing tires. (Rough kids, but very environmentally minded.)

12. There are only a few teens left in town who still have their sanity. Those few have seized the day and scheduled a huge (and completely unauthorized) skate rally for 11 days from now. Underage skate rats will be flooding in from all over the state.

13. And rumors are flying that higher authorities (FBI, CIA, SMERSH, Bureau 13) are being called in.

Wow. Will be very careful not to give Binary Larry any reasons to seek revenge on me.

Later

Early morning. I should be in bed. Have been eavesdropping on the following conversation:

MOM: Yeah, so, E, could you work on Raven's programming and get her back over to Bebe's right away? She seemed very concerned about some dusting that needed to get done.

EVILONE: Well, I actually might have some bad news for Bebe about that.

M: Really? I thought that stuff was super easy for you.

EO: Oh, it's not that. I just think Raven's kind of at the end of her life span, you know? Might be time to . . . you know . . . "retire" her.

M: Uh . . . you mean . . . ? OH. "RETIRE" her. Won't that be kind of hard to explain to Bebe? Not to mention your . . . um, twin?

EO: [Laughing evilly.] No. Not hard at all.

Oh the unspeakable evil!!!!!!!!

Later

Raven and I are holed up in the treehouse for safety. Retire MY golem, huh? Let her try.

165

—Uh, I hope she doesn't try it tonight. I have no idea how I would stop her.

June 21

golems protecting me from danger, 0; golems being protected by me, 0; scenes of pure evil interrupted just in time, 1

Woke up in the treehouse and Raven was not there. Quickly searched the downstairs, then fake-lurched my way up to the bedroom, only to interrupt this charming scene:

EVILONE: Now pick up the chainsaw with your right hand.

RAVEN: K.

EO: Now use the chainsaw to cut off your head.

R: [Starting to obey.] K.

ME: [Busting in.] WHAT THE RUDDERTRUCKING? RAVEN, PUT THAT CHAINSAW DOWN!

R: K.

EO: What the jimjars?!?!? Raven's not supposed to obey you. Have you been messing with her programming?

ME: Of course she's supposed to obey ME! I'm as much Emily as you are!

EO: [Snorting.] Oh yeah? Look, Raven's dangerous, I'm gonna retire her, and you can't stop me.

ME: GAHHHHHHHH!!!!! [Kicking her in the back of the knee with my cast.]

EO: OOF! OW! [Hauling herself off the floor and tackling me.] BFF! BFF! BFF! UHHHH!

ME: ARRRRRRRRRRRRAVEN GET HER OFF ME!

EO: [Dangling from Raven's powerful grip.] RAVEN! LET ME DOWN! [Sprinting to the sun-spigot. Cranking it up full force. Turning the hose toward ME.]

ME: RAVEN, GET ME OUT OF HEEEEEEEERE!

Raven grabbed me and dove out the window, sliding down the drainpipe while I clutched her for dear life. EvilOne ran to the window and started shouting after us as we fled, but I covered Raven's ears with my hands and chanted "Bobby Brady Bobby Brady Bobby Brady" until we were well away. Unbelievable depths of evil!!!!!!! Have taken Raven to the secret sewer. Am very grateful EvilOne does not know about it. Will have to either find myself some other kind of protection that cannot be used against me, or rely on myself for my safety!

Later

Have left Raven in the sewer. Am now slinking around the mostly deserted streets of Silifordville, clutching FakeCat for comfort, and feeling bleak and afeard. Am using stealth tactics so that no police see me. You never know what a police officer may consider "artistic." Black dress, a homemade stuffed black cat, and a cast painted to match? It's the paddy wagon for you, kiddo!

—Uh, I guess I really have no right acting like the martyr here, since I am actually responsible for hundreds of mental-health cases and artist interrogations.

Also: have caught myself with my finger up my nose three times today. GAH!!!!!!!!

Later

Have noticed a big increase in loonies out on the streets tonight compared to the past few days. A quick visit to the Silifordville hospital has explained it: They just don't have room for everyone. Seems like the doctors have started releasing the slightly less spastic ones. This includes a lot of teens, apparently. I observed a large group of them congregating in a parking lot outside a grocery store. (Typical teen behavior that I have never understood. It seems extremely unfun.)

They seemed subdued, depressed, and slightly zombielike.
—OK, on the other hand, this is ALSO somewhat typical teen behavior. Perhaps they have actually been cured. Hard to say.

Am headed back to the sewer. Will have to sleep there for safety!

Later—in the sewer

Am glad I brought Victorian tapestries down here. They make reasonably good sleeping bags.

June 22

bizarre conversation units, |||; new depths of evil discovered, |

Have had a somewhat disturbing encounter with Binary Larry. Was hanging out in the secret sewer, painting on my mural, when my section suddenly took a turn to the south. I wanted to keep painting—I mean, I was getting to something good there—but I'd made that deal with him that south walls were his. So I put down my brush and went in search of him.

He's never too hard to find what with his squeeky boom box and all. (Squeeky Boom Box = great name for a band.)

Our conversation went a little bit like this:

Squeeky Boombox

ME:	Binary Larry.
BINARY LARRY:	WASSSSSSSUH. November December.
ME:	[?????] Uh, yeah. Can I trade you a north wall for a south wall? It's important to my mural.
BL:	Sure thing, NovDec.
ME:	Are you calling me "NovDec"?
BL:	November December. I heard that's your new nickname.
ME:	WHAT NOW? Where did you hear that?
BL:	My man Froggy, he told me you're taking down June July.
ME:	[Slight bleeding from brain.] WHAT IN GACK'S NAME ARE YOU TALKING ABOUT?

Long story short: When not at home making MY life miserable, EvilOne has apparently been battling the current Ms. Popularity, a girl named June July (Yeah. No joke. Her sister's named Nicole Penny) for . . . popularity. POPULARITY. Kids have started calling EvilOne November December, and it sounds like she's a pretty strong contender for the throne.

Had to choke back barf as I was listening to all this. Also, am having trouble believing that someone who is even 50% Emily Strange would go after popularity.

Unless . . .

Unless popularity serves her evil motives, that is.

Binary Larry doesn't seem at all perturbed that I'm apparently leading two wildly different lives. I could tell him there's this evil version of me running around, BUT, I can foresee all the tiresome sentences it would take me to explain the whole complex mess to him, and would rather just let things be.

Per Binary Larry, "I" rank as follows with the skate crowd:

1. #2 most hardcore skater in town (!!!!) —second only to local legend Fishballs, who has ruled for the past 5 years.
2. #1 best at naming new tricks.
3. #1 most creative swearing.
4. #13 best hair.
5. #3 best dressed.
6. #1 best at modifying skateboards.
7. #1 quickest with revenge noogies, headlocks, groin kicks, and insults.
8. #1 most knowledgeable about punk bands that existed before anyone's parents were born.
9. #3 most well-supplied with spray paint.
10. #1 most willing to use spray paint on public surfaces.
11. #5 best tattoos. (Since when do we have tattoos?)
12. #4 most fun, and rising. (Since when do we have fun with people?)
13. #3 best conversationalist. (Since when do we have conversations with people?)

I feel . . . weird inside.

Later

OK—as if the night has not been unsettling enough, I just had Bizarre Conversation #2 with Binary Larry. My mural had taken yet another turn, this time onto a west-facing wall. Went in search of him one more time. Our chat was as follows:

ME:	Dude, sorry, can I take a west wall?
BINARY LARRY:	A west wall, uh, uh, uh, the thing is, I need those walls.
ME:	You need them?
BL:	We had an agreement, man.
ME:	K, that's cool. [Turning to go.]
BL:	Hey, wait a minute, I gotta ask you something.
ME:	[Turning back.] [Waiting for his question.]
BL:	[Sweating.] [Gulping.] Here's the thing. The thing is . . .
ME:	[Waiting . . .]
BL:	The thing is, I think you're . . . . cool. And, so, like, if I told you something . . . really, really secret . . . about the west walls, would you promise me you would, y'know, never act on that knowledge?
ME:	[Heart filling with a greedy, panicky joy of

curiosity. Preparing smooth, reassuring lie so BL would spill his information.] . . . No.

BL: [Taken aback.] No? You wouldn't promise me?

ME: [Flustered.] Wait, that's not what I wanted to say at all. I meant to say, uh . . . guh . . . plugh . . . I mean . . . C'mon, just tell me, man, PLEEEEEASE!

BL: [Giving me extremely weirded-out look.] First promise!

ME: Yuh . . . nuh . . . I can't!

BL: [Cold look in his eyes.] Forget you, man, the west walls are mine.

Later

Crawled out of the sewers and slunk home. Raven and I are now hunkered down in bushes outside my house. Am shocked and disappointed that I could not pull off the simplest of lies. How hard would it have been to say "Yes"? When the rewards were obviously rich? When I cannot afford to make Binary Larry, of all people, mad at me? WHAT IS WRONG WITH ME?

Also, WHAT IS UP WITH THE WEST WALLS?

Later

Went inside for sandwich provisions and ran into the kitchen without proper concern for booby traps. Was painfully shocked by an electrified metal plate in front of the refrigerator. EvilOne will SUFFER!!!!!!!!!

OK, back to the sewer.

June 23
booby traps set, 0; sewer secrets discovered, 0

Woke up at nightfall and snuck home. Hid in the bushes until I saw EvilOne leave, then crept in (CAREFULLY). (Side note: Had better get things settled at home soon. Am spending way too much time hiding in bushes.) Spent some time attempting to come up with painful and/or humiliating booby trap for EvilOne, but it went nowhere. Finally settled for downloading pictures of EvilOne screaming at her blond hair in the mirror. It really DOES pay to install hidden video cameras in every room of your home! Then I programmed the Oddisee so that the pictures would pop up on the screen every five minutes. Also papered bedroom walls with large printouts of said photos. Am hoping she takes them down promptly. They give me the heebie-jeebies.

OK—am out of here—cannot afford to have her catch me here!

Later
Back in the secret sewer. Have begun my investigation of the west walls. They look exactly like all the other walls. Have thumped them and heard nothing unusual. Exploration was cut short

by prompt arrival of Binary Larry. Am now noticing that he almost always shows up about ten minutes after I do, regardless of the time of night. Have apologized to him about last night as best I could. He seemed ready to forgive and forget, but not to give up information about the west walls. We mostly left each other alone except when he came to ask me for a safety pin.

ME:	Yeah, I have safety pins. What size?
BINARY LARRY:	It's for my shirt. I lost a button.
ME:	[Taking miscellaneous items out of pockets and spreading them out. Looking for button-sized safety pin.]
BL:	You are the girl with Everything Possible in her pockets.

ME:	You don't even know. OK, here you go—hey, cool buttons.
BL:	Thanks. They're kind of sentimental too. I'm hating that I lost one.
ME:	[Silently making mental notes on BL's cool buttons. Should find or craft him a replacement. Must try to get back in his good graces.]

Later—at home, getting provisions

Snuck into the house very cautiously, but EvilOne is nowhere to be seen. She's been spending a lot of time out of the house lately. Am hoping she is working on her grand popularity takeover and not her grand plan to preemptively destroy me. Am now sitting nice and cozy at the Oddisee and trying to work on plans for A) reversal of psychic damage to townspeople, and B) solution to my doppelgänger problem.

Cats have been walking casually into the bedroom, seeing me at the Oddisee, hissing, and running away. Is not helping my self-esteem any. Am clutching FakeCat for some small comfort. Is not helping my typing any.

Later

OK. I am getting nothing accomplished because A) pictures of blond EvilOne keep popping up and making me laugh, and B) I cannot stop obsessing over where EvilOne is and what mischief she is up to. Have never in my life given so much thought to another person and it does not sit well. Let me state again that she will feel my wrath.

Later

Have thought it over and am not really sure what irreplaceable skills I have to make EvilOne hesitate before doing away with me. Here's a short list of what I've got that she doesn't:

1. Tendency to cry whenever I think of the hopelessness of getting rid of EvilOne. Or when I see a sad commercial on TV. Or when someone looks at me funny.
2. Guitar skills. Must remember my guitar skills.
3. Crippling need for cat affection.
4. Basic respect for my mother and my golem.
5. Strong need for solitude/intolerance of people.
6. Seeming inability to lie. Very inconvenient.
7. Working knowledge of Great-Aunt Millie.
8. Enjoyment of a good, terrifying nightmare.
9. Desire to spend evenings painting a sewer rather than doing something useful, like getting rid of EvilOne.
10. Artistic talent, based on the fact that EvilOne didn't do a single drawing in my journal in two days.
11. Um.
12. . . .
13. OK, well, art skills, guitar skills, Great-Aunt Millie . . .

Will cling to those for now.

Later

VERY close call a few minutes ago when I heard EvilOne's footsteps on the stairs. Had to throw my cast out the window and jump after it. Am reluctant to go back to the sewer. I miss the comforts of home, man. Am once more hiding in the bushes near the house, trying to get tough with myself and figure out how all this is going to end.

13 Ways All This Could End:

1. One of us dies.
2. One of us leaves.
3. We both stay, but she agrees to bleach her hair again and keep out of my room.
4. I wake up in the hospital, having been in the grips of a terrible fever dream for the past 17 days.
5. One of us is adopted by Gigi and Bebe. (Hopefully EvilOne.)
6. My mother reveals her diabolical prank on me.
7. My holodeck session ends.
8. A more interesting drama arises and we forget to be enemies.
9. Every other human being on Earth is suddenly vaporized in an extreme solar event, and the only reason we are saved is that we're holed up in the sunproof bedroom, and

we agree to each take one hemisphere of the world as our private territory.

10. I program Raven to kidnap EvilOne, knock her unconscious, drive her across the country, and leave her in some random town.

11. EvilOne and I make an appearance on a talk show and let the audience decide our fate.

12. EvilOne and I hug and learn.

13. We are both killed by a natural disaster of some sort. You know: global flood, asteroid hitting the Earth, return of the dinosaurs . . . I might prefer this to hugging and learning.

Later

I AM BRILLIANT!

Maybe.

The Ratts and the 12th Street Toughs are vandalizing all of the town's cars tonight. Am going to frame EvilOne for doing it. (Somehow.) Then will turn her in to the police. With any luck, she will be locked away long enough for me to make a plan to neutralize her FOREVER!!!!!

Am headed back to the sewer for Raven.

Later

I hid my cast in yet another friendly clump of bushes, then Raven and I roamed the town, and she videotaped me pretending to knife tires. Am on top of the world!

Never underestimate the power of positive revenge!

Later—almost dawn

I could not face another day of sleeping in the sewer, so I snuck into the house and woke Mom up. Begged her to let me hide out in her room for the day and not to tell my doppelgänger. She said OK, but there was a lot of eye-rolling. She clearly does not see the danger I am in!

June 24
royal disasters, 1; strategies for extricating self, 0

Yobbing hamdacks, what a mess!!!!!

Was woken up at noon by a very upset Mom. Came out to find police, Venus Fang Fang, Bebe, Raven, and EvilOne sitting in the living room.

Everyone was yelling at once, but eventually I got the following sorted out:

1. Some concerned townsperson videotaped Raven videotaping me knifing tires last night.
2. But of course, everyone thinks it was EvilOne because I wasn't wearing a cast.
3. Venus Fang Fang also videotaped EvilOne doing some extravagant vandalism of her fence last night.

4. But of course, everyone thinks it was me because EvilOne WAS wearing a cast.
5. EvilOne and I are both taking the Fifth.
6. I was somehow introduced to everyone as "Jemily," while EvilOne got to go by "Emily." Grrrr!

7. I feel, and hope EvilOne feels, that I got her better than she got me.

8. But I am not happy that she must now know my leg is healed.

9. There has been no mention of the ill-fated ribbon-cutting ceremony or any link to either of us.

10. Bebe has been sternly reprimanded for not keeping Raven under better control.

11. If Raven is caught in mischief again, she is looking at some time spent in institutional learning facilities.

12. EvilOne is probably not going to be incarcerated, which is bad, but she's looking at some heavy community service: namely, personally replacing hundreds of knifed tires. Which is good. It should keep her occupied for a while.

13. And I have been sentenced to repaint Venus Fang Fang's fence, starting in half an hour SHARP.

Sounds mild, but A) it's a very long fence, and B) I have done my tour of duty with white paint for the year, thank you very much, and C) the worst part is, it looks like Venus Fang Fang is planning to supervise me the whole time. Oh no, pardon me, that's not even the worst part. The worst part is that D) Venus Fang Fang is a TALKER. Is there anything more poisonous than a talker? No. No, there isn't. Unless it's that E) the talker is supervising someone who is not a talker. Namely me.

Hours later

I no longer feel that EvilOne is getting the worse punishment.
Here is a brief rundown of things I did in eight hours at Venus
Fang Fang's house today:

1. Unwillingly heard well-meant piece of useless advice on
   life from Venus Fang Fang—345 million, zillion times.
2. Wished for death, or at least sudden deafness—345
   million, zillion times.
3. Smudged self with nasty stinky white paint—23 times.
4. Wished that paint smelled more like freshly baked
   cinnamon rolls—35 times.
5. Amused self by silently saying the word "paint" until it
   lost all meaning—84,572,957 times.
6. Pondered clever and excruciating revenge for EvilOne—111
   times.
7. Hoped that Venus Fang Fang might suddenly succumb to
   laryngitis—48 times.
8. Excused self to take extended bathroom break—13 times.
9. Responded to Venus Fang Fang's advice on managing my
   overactive bladder—0 times.
10. Responded "No fangs, I'm good," when asked if I wanted a
    snack—2 times.
11. Cheered self by reflecting that I was indirectly gaining
    valuable karate skills—7 times.
12. Wished for Tom Sawyer to come by so I could trick him

into taking over my work—once.

13. Hoped that black cats might come along and mark freshly painted white fence as their territory—4 times.

On the upside, as I've mentioned, Venus Fang Fang has a very strong accent of some sort, which made for unintentional comedy when she told me that she is the autha of a book called <u>Defeating Your Enema</u>. That was when I spoke two of my four sentences of the day.

ME: Why would an enema need defeating?
                       You could just . . . not use it.
VENUS FANG FANG: Your ENEMA, chald, your NAMESIS,
                       your ADVARSARY.

Pretty funny . . . Also, note to self: Tomorrow, must see if I can get Venus Fang Fang sidetracked into giving me some advice on defeating MY enemy. It probably has to do with defeating the enemy inside you, or hugging and learning, or some such nonsense, but it's worth a shot. After all, this IS a woman who managed to disable a Vanian-Jugg circuit and whose backyard alarm system gave me pause for, like, a full fifteen minutes.

OK, am going to the sewer to sleep.

Later—nighttime at last!

Hid in my favorite bushes outside our house and waited for EvilOne to leave, then snuck in and went up to my bedroom. Triggered some kind of tripwire on the staircase, and several million thumbtacks shot out at me. Grabbling frumdarks!!!!!!!!

Later

Have been enjoying some alone time in the room, tinkering with the Oddisee and checking on my plants. Man, I loooooooooove my lovely room. Cannot believe EvilOne has me on the run. Have GOT to come up with brilliant plan to get her out of my world.

Magic 8 Ball has not been a ton of help lately, but I can't help reaching for it at times like this . . .

Hmm. I just asked the 8 Ball, "What should I do about EvilOne?" and its answer was, "SPIRIT ELDERS HOLD THE ANSWERS!"

Bizarre! Am headed upstairs to visit Great-Aunt Millie.

Later

Am dumbfounded at the depths of the evil of the EvilOne!!!!!!!!

It was obvious that EvilOne had been up in the attic already. Looks like she had some kind of temper tantrum and splashed black paint all over the place. It took me a long time to find Great-Aunt Millie. I finally noticed a barrel full of broken glass and dead leaves that had no business being there. I tipped it over and scrabbled through the broken glass until I found Great-Aunt Millie.

She wasn't good. She couldn't even talk. I pulled her out of the glass and tried to give her a little comfort if I could by cradling her in my arms. I had to be very gentle to get her to relax on my lap. She was not too visible anymore except for a shimmer in the air like heat writhing. Occasionally a face sharpened up out of the shimmering air. You could see the resemblance to me, and to Patti, and maybe even to Mystery, if I'm going to be honest.

I asked her what happened, tried so hard to give her a little of my energy if that would help. And we did manage to communicate a bit. I knew I wasn't really hearing her with my ears or seeing her with my eyes; it was all a direct feed into my brain from her essential energy, still vital enough to present herself in a way I could understand.

It mostly came into my mind in emotions and images, like this: EvilOne's anger at not knowing about Great-Aunt Millie. EvilOne coming up to the attic, leading Raven, who was carrying the barrel of broken glass. EvilOne trapping Great-Aunt Millie in a net made of . . . rage, I think, and burying her in the barrel. Then more raging outside the barrel. And Great-Aunt Millie getting weaker and weaker inside.

I was getting kind of enraged myself at all of this and just hating, hating, hating EvilOne—for her evil, and for making me feel helpless to stop her, and for being so alien and incomprehensible.

Why can't she just be the OtherMe I thought she was—someone I can understand and agree with perfectly, all the time? But Great-Aunt Millie seemed to be telling me I was wrong about EvilOne, that we are the SAME. So I tried to show her all our differences, all the memories and skills and qualities we didn't share. But Great-Aunt Millie seemed to be saying that I was looking at it all wrong. And then this image popped into my head, a blurry, cross-eyed image of me and EvilOne that kept sort of trying to pull together, but never succeeded.

It started to give me a headache, and then it faded away.

Super frustrated, I asked Great-Aunt Millie out loud what I was supposed to do.

And she seemed to be telling me that if I really wanted to solve my problems with EvilOne, all we needed to do was Hug and Learn.

SIGH.

So much for that lead.

After that, Great-Aunt Millie didn't try to talk, just looked at me, so real, full of physics and energy touching my brain.

I put her in a shoe box and hid her in the basement. Will do some reading on ways to rehabilitate poltergeists and see what I can do for her.

And I don't care if we are the same—EvilOne will paaaaayyyy!

Later

Have just finished a difficult conversation with Mom. I found her in the living room with Mystery curled up on her lap. It was the first time I've EVER seen Mystery on someone else's lap. Ohhhhhhhh how it hurt.

ME: [Head high. Holding tight to my dignity.] Hey, Patti, time for some straight talk.

MOM: [Putting Mystery down, sort of sheepishly.] What's up, E?

ME: Just wanted you to know what the other Emily has been doing lately. She tried to destroy Raven, she's tried to kill me a few times, and I just found Great-Aunt Millie buried in a barrel of broken glass. She seems to be spending a lot of time outside the house, and I have no idea what she's up to. So . . . if you happen to have a small knife or other weapon you could conceal on your person from now on, I'd recommend it.

M: Oh, is THAT why you've been sleeping in my closet?

ME: Yes! Are you even listening to me? We're all in

danger here! You could be next!

M: Sure, sure, I'm listening. You're going through a tough patch right now. I remember when I was young, my sister and I fought all the time.

ME: Oh my gobfarks. We are NOT sisters.

M: Well . . . no, you're not sisters per se, but you're both my daughters, and I'm sorry to see that you're having all this conflict.

ME: [Ugly suspicions dawning.] Uh, Patti, are you saying that . . . you . . . LOVE . . . the other Emily?

M: Well of course, I love both of you.

ME: AIIEEIIEIIEEEE!!!!!!!

M: Hey, come on, remember what we promised the neighbors about screaming?

Cannot BELIEVE this!!!! I don't see how she can love that evil thing! I mean, this is a girl who watches with pleasure while the cats torment small creatures in the yard. I/We didn't used to be like that. A month ago, I would have rescued the mouse/snake/cockroach, doctored its wounds (or reanimated it as some kind of unholy golem, if I'd been too late), and released it into the wild. And scolded the cats. Now their torture sessions drag on and end tragically while EvilOne stands by, totally absorbed in the cruel spectacle. And I've read enough stories of true crime to know the signs of a future serial killer when I see them.

189

OK. Well, serial killer or not, she's a vile creature without merit and I can't believe Mom loves her!!!!!!!!!!!!

Although. OK. To be totally honest, I have been feeling more and more like I am a sappy spineless creature without merit. And Mom said she loves me too.

Although to be TOTALLY honest I really don't think she sounded as sincere about the whole loving either of us thing as she used to before we got duplicated.

Later

Have done some research and filled Great-Aunt Millie's shoe box with almond blossoms, ectoplasmic white goo, red feathers, and a bar of Ivory soap.

Am exhausted by hard daytime labor and emotional night. Going to bed. In the sewer.

June 25
sunblock units, 123; useful bits of advice gathered, 11

If I may add one more terrible thing about my punishment at Venus Fang Fang's house, it's that it takes place during daylight hours. Am sleep-deprived and sick to death of the sun.

However, on the plus side, I have cunningly directed the topic of Venus Fang Fang's unrelenting monologue toward defeating one's ~~enema~~ enemy. If she is surprised to hear me asking lots of questions after yesterday's four sentences, she is not letting on. Have not told her why I want to know, specifically. And, MAN, she knows a lot. For example, she very casually told me a little-known refinement on recruiting false-flag agents, how to break a common sleeper hold with both hands tied, and some of the finer points of coercion, extortion, and blackmail.

It's sounding like she may actually, in her youth, back in the day, have been involved in the training of spies, or something like that. Hence the incredible obstacle course in her backyard. Am pondering how I could possibly sign myself up for some kind of spy training with her. Well, one more day of painting to go, so I'd better come up with an idea pronto.

Later

Saw a fairly disturbing spectacle on my way home: a bunch of teens all wearing black, walking single file down the street. There was something very . . . I don't know, just OFF about them, so I snuck around in front of them and hid so I could watch them closely as they passed. Can safely say I do not think they have been cured. These were NOT your average mournful teens, mad at the world because they spent a little time in a mental hospital. For starters, they all seemed

GONE BATTY

to have the same distinct body language, and were slinking along in this kind of defiant-aggressive-cocky-yet-zombie-like manner. Also, they'd all cut the sleeves off their shirts, making a sort of uniform effect. Ugh! I've seen teens suffer from the crushing need to be like their friends, but I've never seen it look so creepy!!

Should really get that antidote made!!!!!

Later—nighttime

Ate dinner with Mom and EvilOne. We barely spoke. Tension was high. Afterward, I ran down to the basement without proper caution for booby traps and got a mouthful of spiderwebs as my reward. GUH! I will be spitting for the next week!! Tried to think of a foolproof barrier to keep EvilOne out for a bit while I checked on Great-Aunt Millie, but ended up just pushing a chair in front of the door.

Anyway. All of the almond blossoms, ectoplasmic white goo, and red feathers are gone, and Great-Aunt Millie is looking slightly more energetic. Ivory soap is still there. It has a single bite mark on it. Am assuming it was not to Great-Aunt Millie's tastes. Am removing it.

Am reconsidering keeping Great-Aunt Millie down here in the basement, considering I don't have the booby-trapping skills to keep her safe from EvilOne. I guess I will have to take her to the only truly secure place I know.

Later

Am in the sewer. Have informed Great-Aunt Millie that this will have to be her home until I can neutralize the danger of EvilMe.

Brought better equipment with me this time, and quickly X-rayed all the west walls before Binary Larry showed up—right on time, ten minutes after me. Will develop the films at home . . . Assuming EvilOne is not around, that is.

Later—back at home

EvilOne was nowhere in sight, giving me plenty of time to review the X-rays. Frabbling jellyjars!!!! There is ANOTHER secret sewer behind the one I know about. Binary Larry clearly intends to prevent me from finding it. But WHY? Must get some alone time down there so I can break through.

June 26
fence-painting projects completed, 0; senseis found, 1

Venus Fang Fang surprised the cheeks off me today when I showed up. First, the fence has been completely painted!! She admits to hiring a handyman to finish my work!!!! And now she is asking me what I think about commuting the rest of my sentence to time in what she calls her "abstacle garden." Have been cool about it. Curbed my enthusiasm and told her calmly that I would be OK with that. Am sitting outside waiting for her to change into her trainer's gear. Contrary to appearances, am very excited.

FOREVER Later

Am on break from dire torment in the abstacle garden. Venus Fang Fang began my training with a request that I "take off that sally cast" and not wear it again in her presence. Note to self: No use hiding anything from Venus Fang Fang. She is mistress of deception, and I am hardly at the top of my game. Also, she appears to think I have some kind of behavior problem that is in need of rough treatment. Today has been like one of those terrible tough-love rehab camps,

Before!

without the love. She has been putting me through brutally hard paces in broad sunlight. Am wearing heavy protective gear.

Clearly I should have been more careful about her early impression of me. Would be much further along with her if I'd cultivated more of a delicate flower persona. Would like to get a look at her personal library, for example. Have not been invited inside at all, and I suspect I have some dues to pay before that happens.

Later

HAVE FOUND BINARY LARRY'S SKULL BUTTON.

IN THE MUD OF VENUS FANG FANG'S ABSTACLE GARDEN.

Will have to interrogate him tonight!!!!!!!!!!!!!!!

Later

Have been hanging out in the semi-secret sewer, painting halfheartedly on my mural while trying to plot my strategy with Binary Larry. This whole not-being-able-to-lie thing has put me at an unwelcome disadvantage. Will just have to see where instinct takes me.

After!

Later

Have spoken with Binary Larry. Here's how it went:

BINARY LARRY: Sup, Emily, your mural is shaping up wicked!

ME: Sup. Found your button.

BL: . . . Whoa.

ME: Whoa, indeed. It was in Venus Fang Fang's abstacle, er, obstacle garden.

BL: [Gulping, turning red, and feebly attempting lies.] Who? . . . Oh, her. Oh, uh, you know her?

ME: [Experimentally.] You know I do.

BL: No . . . what . . . I . . . how . . .

ME: You should ask her for some lessons in deception, dude. You're . . . not good.

BL: I have to go now.

AhHhhahhahah!

Will follow him and see what I can discover.

Later

Brain is hemorrhaging slightly.

I tracked Binary Larry as he left the secret sewer. First he went out to the skate park, which I have not visited in weeks,

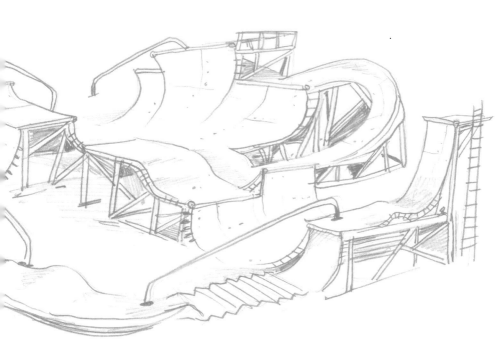

and which now sports a wicked series of ramps, pipes, twisting rails, and mazelike tunnels. I recognized my own carpentry style right away. Well, that explains what EvilOne's been up to. Also, it explains why the local teens thought it might be possible to hold a skate rally in Silifordville. Seriously, kids really ARE going to come from all over for THIS.

Dude, I soooooo miss my skills. Would skate the stuffing out of this place!!!!

Anyway, Binary Larry skated for an hour or so while I spied. (His technique is tolerably good, I guess.) And then he left the skate park. And skated to Venus Fang Fang's house, let himself in, and went to his room. It wasn't until then that I finally recognized

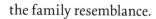

the family resemblance.

Yep.

Binary Larry is Venus Fang Fang's SON.

OBVIOUSLY he is A) not as doofy as he seems, and B) quite possibly as talented at deception as his mother! And OBVIOUSLY, she is using him to keep me from getting into the supersecret sewer!!!

What is she hiding in there?

Will do my best to find out tomorrow.

Later

Back at home. EvilOne was nowhere around, so I took the opportunity to get Raven to move the huge antique birdcage down to the basement. I will barricade myself down here tonight and (hopefully) sleep in some kind of comfort and safety. EvilOne seems preoccupied with Project Popularity, so maybe I'm OK for now.

June 27

senseis interrogated, 1; secrets cunningly dragged out of senseis, 0

Have talked to Venus Fang Fang about Binary Larry. It went a little bit like this:

ME:	So, Venus Fang Fang. I found out about Binary Larry being your son.
VENUS FANG FANG:	Oh yas. Larry told me the two of you paint togather.
ME:	. . . Oh. And . . . you know WHERE we paint?
VFF:	The sewars, I believe?
ME:	Yeah. Um . . . I don't really have any follow-up remarks at this time.
VFF:	Very wall. Let's get on with your endurance training. You're a lattle soft.

SIGH! Clearly I did not have control over that conversation. Maybe tomorrow I will have the nerve to ask her straight out what the two of them are hiding in the super secret sewer. It's just not in me today.

Later

I am no longer worried about EvilOne killing me. Venus Fang Fang's training is sure to do the job first.

On the ~~bright~~ dark side, I get to graduate from daytime to nighttime very soon. Venus Fang Fang is a cruel sensei, but I can't help but admire her brilliance in training me on deadly sunshine first. If I can perform under conditions as adverse as daylight, imagine what I'll be able to accomplish in the lovely dark!

Later

Have had excellent chat with Venus Fang Fang. It started when I said something gloomy and threatening about EvilOne, and continued a little something like this:

VENUS FANG FANG: Now, chald. Your saster seemed nice. She became good friends with Viscer when she was walking him every day.

ME: Oh yeah? She . . . was friends . . . with your dog.

VFF: Samthing wrong?

ME: Just a little . . . brain hemorrhaging is all.

VFF: Look here, Jamily. I can understand hastility toward your twin. What is not making sense is the note of stunned disbelief I'm picking up. Why would it sarprise you that she enjoyed walking my dog? Is this the first sammer you've spent with her?

ME: . . . You're not the dumbest adult I've ever met, Venus Fang Fang.

VFF: Wall, thank you. You're not the dumbest chald I've met. Now do you want to answer my quastion?

208

ME: No, because you wouldn't believe the answer.

VFF: I may sarprise you. I am so good at telling the dafference between truth and lie, I may as well be psychic.

ME: Um, I hate to contradict you, but you just said my saster, er, sister, seemed "nice." I'm afraid she's got you pretty well bamboozled.

VFF: Indaeed. I did say she SEEMED NICE.

ME: [Slowly gaining small hope of being understood.] Oh . . . kay. So then I guess you won't have a problem believing that until twenty days ago I was an only child, and that I accidentally duplicated myself using a device I built from items found in a junk-shop Dumpster?

VFF: . . . . [Chewing on this.] . . . . [Clearly deciding to believe it.] . . . . [Against all odds.] . . . . You ARE an interasting chald.

ME: Also, my duplicate got all my skateboarding, lying, booby-trapping, and booby-trap-evading skills, and left me with crying spells, nose-picking, a crippling need for feline affection, and a self-esteem problem.

VFF: That axplains . . . Naver mind. If it makes you feel any batter, no one should have been able to get through my fence alarm.

ME: Awww ... no offense, Venus Fang Fang, but that's kid stuff. I mean, your alarm was the best I've seen, but I DO practice.

VFF: You don't understand what I'm rally telling you, because you have no idea just whose yard you broke into. I happen to be the world's foremost axpert in tradecraft for covert operations.

ME: [That ... is ... so ... cool ...] Fancy that.

VFF: And when I say no one should have been able to get through, I mean that my most phenomenally talented student, a stanningly good-looking thirty-seven-year-old prafessional defyer of death and mocker of defenses, tested it for me. HE couldn't get through it, but YOU, a tharteen-year-old with no formal training, got through 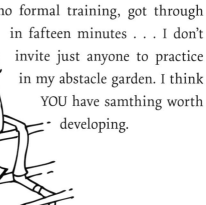 in fafteen minutes . . . I don't invite just anyone to practice in my abstacle garden. I think YOU have samthing worth developing.

ME:	Huh . . . [OK. Feeling slightly better about self.] So why doesn't it look like you've trained anyone here in, I don't know, fourteen years?
VFF:	Wall, I'm actually retired. I had to stop because of the blood already on my hands.
ME:	[Thinking back to my last burger.] I know how you feel.
VFF:	And I vowed to stop creating killars.
ME:	Venus Fang Fang?
VFF:	Yes, Jamily?
ME:	First thing is, I hate being called Jamily, so could you cut that out? Second thing, the highest respect I can show you is the truth, which is that the girl you know as Emily is evil beyond belief and must be eliminated before she murders me, my mother, or my golem. Third, I seem to have lost some of my key skills in defeating the enema, er, enemy, so can you train me to defeat her if I promise there will be no killing?
VFF:	Can you pramise there will be no violence at all?
ME:	Sure, as long as your next sentence does not mention hugging and/or learning . . . Oh, and fourth, what's your deal with violence?

I let myself in for it there, for real. Had to endure an hour-long lecture, which boiled down to the fact that Venus Fang Fang has had some bad, bad experiences with violence, none of which (unfortunately) she would describe in detail for me. But clearly she has strong personal evidence that violence is, like, really bad. So, bless her heart, she retired from the spy business when Young Larry was born, and has spent the past fourteen years fine-tuning her philosophy of defeating the enemy through non-violent means.

And so, as my first task, she wants ME to stop all fisticuffs with EvilOne. Chaaaaa! She thinks I'M the guilty one??????

Later

Have looked back at journal entries and clearly I AM the guilty one. As evidenced by the scuffle of June 14. Why would any reasonably badass defyer of death and mocker of defenses go and punch someone in the face WHILE MOSTLY PARALYZED??????? That's just . . . not bright. Oh, and let's also refer to the tussle of June 21, which I instigated by kicking my double with MY FULL-LEG CAST. Am disappointed in self at the moment.

Later

Note to self: If I am ever in need of self-worth again, should remind myself that Venus Fang Fang, world's foremost spy trainer, wants to train ME!!!!!!!!!!!!!!!

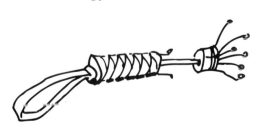

June 28

Am getting less soft. Spent a lot of time working on endurance in the abstacle garden. Have not yet met the goal Venus Fang Fang set for me. Need to shave another three minutes off my time. Maybe tomorrow. Finally we moved on to Locks 101. I picked every lock

on Venus Fang Fang's practice door; then replaced each one with a new lock of my own design. She told me it was a good effort and cracked all five of my locks in one minute flat.

Also, to supplement my growing skills, Venus Fang Fang has called in an expert on devices. Her name is Queenie Kew. I find her tedious and have had to forbid her to explain how her devices work. At least that way I can enjoy them for a couple minutes. Their real, intended functions may not cause them to spectacularly self-destruct like the functions I invent for them,

Some of Queenie Kew's devices, post-Me.

but flatting bugrits, hearing Queenie Kew explain ANYTHING makes me so tired.

Next came a crash course in Advanced Empathy. Venus Fang Fang says that I have all the mechanical abilities I need to make (or defuse) excellent booby traps, but that I'm clueless when it comes to predicting what the enemy will do next, which is critical to primo booby-trapping skills. So, my lameness with booby traps essentially stems from my inability to understand the enemy. I can feel that, all right. I definitely don't understand EvilOne. Submitted to two hours of emotionally draining empathy practice. Am glad it's over.

It's OK, though. I need the help. I KNOW I used to be good at this stuff. Blast EvilOne for taking my skills!!!! Hanging out with Venus Fang Fang and Queenie Kew is painful but necessary, in the way that relearning to walk after breaking every bone in your body is painful but necessary.

In other news, I caught myself with my finger up my nose three times today.

Later—back at home

Came home real pooped tonight, but AT LEAST I did not race upstairs to my bedroom with no thought for booby traps. Was able to detect and defuse a stink bomb inside the doorknob. Am extremely proud of self and grateful to Venus Fang Fang. When I finally, safely opened the door, EvilOne looked up expectantly at me through her gas mask, then glowered when she saw there was no stinky cloud. We said nothing. I grabbed some bedding and went to sleep in the birdcage.

June 29
locks picked, 23; codes cracked, 123; satellites hacked, 3

Venus Fang Fang says I am racing through the basic levels of espionage tradecraft and making her pull out her best tricks. Am feeling self-worthy again.

Tonight she analyzed my night vision. I can distinguish sixty-seven more shades of gray than the average person. It seems my eyes just have more rods than most people's do. Who knew? Anyway, she says we can stick to night work from now on. YESSSSSSSSSSS. I am back to sleeping days.

Later

Excellent night of training. Am feeling much better equipped to take on EvilOne. Here are a few of the best lessons Venus Fang Fang has taught me:

1. Winning arguments while making it seem like you're resolving differences.
2. Developing a very sensitive nose for traps, tricks, double crosses, and deception of many kinds.

3. Thinking up and implementing traps, tricks, double crosses, and deception that will be undetectable by your enemy because of her hidden psychological weaknesses.
4. Cobbling together said traps and tricks in a pinch using common household objects.
5. Ferreting out said hidden psychological weaknesses in your enemy.
6. Making allies and cultivating their willingness to do you favors.
7. Developing your powers of intuition and persuasion. (Though the way Venus Fang Fang does it, it's more like ESP and mind control.)
8. Wiring, splicing, soldering, gauging, calibrating . . . I am already an advanced student in this department, but Venus Fang Fang does have some nice techniques that I've picked up.
9. Creating superior diversions.
10. Disguising oneself effectively. (We have not covered accents. Accents are not one of Venus Fang Fang's strengths.)
11. Speedy maneuvering through fiendishly difficult abstacle gardens.
12. Surviving in wilderness settings. (A wilderness-survival arena is one of the many large areas in her massive backyard.)
13. Avoiding physical confrontations.

Later

Have learned from Queenie Kew that Venus Fang Fang is not only the world's foremost expert on spy training, but is also renowned for inventing the spy diaper. This is a little item a spy wears on extended stakeouts, or long interrogations, or whenever it would be counterstrategic to take a bathroom break. Was pleasantly appalled by the thought, and clearly it showed on my face.

QUEENIE KEW: Don't give her THAT look when she offers you one. She'll be terribly ansal—er, insulted.

ME: [Now UNpleasantly appalled.] Why's she going to offer ME a spy diaper?

QK: Because she's PROUD of it! And as a token of her esteem! Come on, you've had SOME empathy training! What are you, new?

ME: Oh. Right. [Secretly planning to diplomatically turn down offers of the spy diaper.]

Note: Spy Diaper = great name for . . . the right kind of band.

Later

Bad stuff! Very bad stuff!

Venus Fang Fang had left me with Queenie Kew for a refresher course on Advanced Explosives, and when she came back there was an ominous expression on her face. She took me aside for a chat and the news was not good. Not good at all. It seems that Binary Larry was at the skate park earlier tonight, and EvilOne (AKA November December, who as far as he knows is ME) was brutally mean to him. He will not tell his mother what was said, but apparently he left the park in deep shame. Venus Fang Fang knows it was not me, but is a great believer in letting chaldren (not to mention spies-in-training) work out their problems on their own, and thought it best to let me explain it to him myself. Great. What fun it will be convincing Binary Larry that I have an evil twin. Really should have cleared this up before now.

He was refusing to answer any of his mother's knocks on his door, so I said my goodbyes and went straight to the sewer in hopes he would show up. No sign of him!! I spent the rest of the night working on my mural. I think it's done, finally. And it's definitely beautiful, though possibly lacking an ounce or two of heart/soul/dark power/aching haunting depth/etc. At least I can take a small (very small) consolation in reflecting that this is MUCH better than anything EvilOne could produce. Although . . . I can't help thinking that if I had just a drop of her evil, my mural would be the better for it.

Interesting!

Later

Have been to the skate park for some spying. Hobbling lintcakes!!!! Things are not all fun and games with EvilOne's popularity power play. I now understand the sinister body language and ripped-off sleeves

I witnessed on those teens four days ago. Their ~~outfits~~ uniforms have progressed into something all too recognizable.

So. It wasn't enough that she warped their minds with our Strangeness, but now she has to zombify them into DRESSING like us? And perform synchronized skateboarding routines at her bidding?

Am filled with eXtreme horror at this scene.

Will fix things here if it's the last thing I do!

Later—daylight—in treehouse—half asleep

Have just woken myself up with the realization that—OK—clearly I've completely forgotten that Venus Fang Fang is Mistress of Deception! If her training has accomplished nothing else, it

has given me a severe case of hero worship, distracting me from whatever is hidden in the super secret sewer. I should have spent all those unsupervised hours last night inspecting the west walls for ways in, and I didn't even think about it!!!!

Still no leads on what might be in there, but here are my top guesses:

1. Enough lethal nerve gas to destroy all human life on Earth. (DELIGHTFULLY HORRIFIC!!!!!)
2. The Ark of the Covenant, Golden Fleece, Holy Grail, Andvarinaut, wreck of the Titanic, or some other relic likely to fetch pots of money at auction.
3. Pots of money.
4. First-edition copies of <u>Defeating Your Enema</u> (with typo).
5. The suspiciously absent Mr. Fang Fang. Bonus points if he is mummified. HUGE bonus points if he is taxidermied.
6. Spy lab full of prototypes of delectable spy gadgets.
7. Crates and crates of spy diapers.
8. Venus Fang Fang's great-grandmother's china.
9. Refugees.
10. MONSTER MONSTER AIIEEEEEE!
11. Some sort of horrendously unholy summoning chamber for the Dread Cthulhu, or one of his associates.
12. Extra food and water supplies, in case of apocalypse. (Seriously, it had better be something more interesting than this.)
13. Command center from which Venus Fang Fang can

control every . . . uh, traffic signal . . . in ALL OF SILIFORDVILLE!!! Bwwahhh hahha hahhhahah!!!!!
OK, am clearly sleep-deprived. This list is OVER!

June 30
hearts broken and smashed, |; best friends lost forever, |

Am crying my heart out as I write this.   My beloved sweet Mystery is dead.   I found her in the yard, all stiff.   There are no words, etc.   I want to ~~die kill~~ I don't even know.   Mom is crying her heart out too.   No tears from EvilOne.   OF COURSE I suspect she is guilty of this, but she has not taken credit like I would expect her to do.

BUT IF SHE DID HAVE ANYTHING TO DO WITH THIS—
   I don't even know what I will do to her, but it will be THE END of my promise of nonviolence to Venus Fang Fang.
   My mouth is filled with horror and the taste of blood.

Later
Have dragged myself up to my room to look for mementos of Mystery to put in her coffin. Have no heart for this. Have always had a businesslike relationship with Death, but this has put us on very unfriendly terms. Am TOTALLY REJECTING this! Cannot handle it AT ALL!!!!!!

The worst part is that for the last month of Mystery's life there were zero cozy snuggles, zero delightful petting sessions, zero playful romps, and zero sweet meows of love.

I miss my Mystery soooooooooooooooooooooooooooooooooooo oooooooooooooo much.

Three minutes later

I just opened up one of the hidden compartments under the floorboards that EvilOne and I built weeks ago when we were friends. I could have sworn it was the one we used to stash assorted cat-related mementos. Instead I found sixty-seven copies of the Manifesto of Strange in easily portable CD format. I'm sure this is very bad news, but at the moment all I can think of is Mystery, and where EvilOne might have moved her old collars, baby toys, and kitten teeth.

Later

EvilOne just came storming up the stairs, catching me crashed out on the floor in full weeping mode. She yelled, "Have you seen the skateboard?" and was about to search the room, but let me tell you, it was not the right moment for her to be searching the room for the skateboard. I leaped up at her like a mother bear and roared in her face. She stepped back, going, "Whoa, whatever," and hustled downstairs.

Later

Am torn between rage and joy. Mystery is ALIVE!!!!!!!!!!!!!!!!!!! And EvilOne will PAY IN BLOOD for making me think she was dead. I have HAD IT with that evil thing in my house, going after all that I hold dear! She is GOING DOWN!!!!!!!!!!!!!!!!!!!!!

Here's how I found out. I was stumbling aimlessly around my bedroom, crying my heart out, bumping into things blindly in my search for mementos of Mystery, and calling out to the other three cats to come and comfort me for CREPES' SAKE, but of course they were mostly hissing from under the bed at me. It was like sulfuric acid splashed on an open wound to hear them hissing at a time like that, and I just couldn't take it anymore, so I sat down at the cat translator and fired it up. Our conversation went something like this:

ME:	Posse, I really need you to not be hissing at me right now.
MILES, NEECHEE, AND SABBATH:	[Spirited hissing.] [Apparently there is no English translation for hissing.]

217

ME: [Weeping hysterically.] I've had Mystery since I was BORN. I can't handle losing her! Can't one of you come comfort me a little? I'll pay in liver!

N: I do not understand all this crying.

S: Liver?

M: You have not lost Mystery.

ME: Yeah, yeah, yeah, her spirit will always be with me, etcetera. I WANT MY KITTYCAT!!!!

N: She's lying on the kitchen counter.

ME: I know. Mom's making a coffin for her. You guys don't understand, she's DEAD!!!!

M: She is not dead.

ME: Sorry guys, she IS. I found her in the yard, all stiff. You know . . . as in lifeless.

N: Have you forgotten the effects of paramytosilicate extract on mammals?

ME: [Sharp intake of breath.] Are you saying . . .

N: That you have been the victim of a cruel prank? Yes. Now stop trying to pick me up.

S: Liver?

Have calmed myself. Have remembered my training and frozen my face into an expression of deep, hidden pain and stoic resignation. Am going downstairs for a funeral.

Later

Am hanging out in the secret sewer, silently communing with Great-Aunt Millie about the day's events. Have attended Mystery's funeral with Mom and EvilEvilOne. Cried a few dignified tears for the look of the thing, and then Mom and I buried the coffin. For

effect, I piled the heaviest rocks I could find on top of the grave, watching EvilOne's reaction. Not even a flinch! Oh the evil!

Am reeeeeeeeally hoping that EvilOne plans to dig up the coffin. She will regret this!!!!!!!!!!!! (Note to self: Will need a new skateboard. The one I buried in Mystery's coffin will never be rideable again.)

Mystery's stiff but indeed living body is here with me and Great-Aunt Millie. I have about three hours before she wakes up. Have brought her favorite treats and toys with me. Am really hoping she does not hiss and run away.

Am also taking the opportunity to pet her as much as I can, while she's still knocked out!

Later

Have just heard Binary Larry arrive. He has not come around to talk to me. He is over in his wing, painting west walls with lines of code. I should probably go try to explain the whole evil-twin situation, but am too exhausted from emotional ups and downs of the day. Maybe later.

About three hours later

Mystery is awake and unhappy. Have explained that she will be living in the secret sewer for a little while.

Am wondering what EvilOne's motives could have been. Does she just enjoy seeing me and Mom suffer? Would she really harm the cats? And what on earth was she doing with sixty-seven copies of the Manifesto of Strange? I mean . . . this town couldn't get much stranger. So what would she need more copies for?

Unless . . .

Oh no . . .

Could she be planning to spread her evil to other towns?

Am more motivated than ever to eliminate her at any cost!!!!

Later

Am sleeping in the sewer today. Even though I hate sleeping on the concrete, I can't bring myself to leave Mystery. She will not snuggle, but has camped out a few feet away.

brrr

July 1
body parts bruised by concrete floors, 17; revenge plans, ½

Have come up with passable plan for taking down EvilOne. I was walking along, wondering to myself why there were so many skateboarding teens on the streets. To be specific, skateboarding teens who did not look like zombies dressed as ME. And therefore, skateboarding teens who were clearly from out of town. That's when I suddenly realized that the huge, unauthorized, unsupervised skate rally is this evening. Hot on the heels of that idea was the startling insight that, OF COURSE, EvilOne would be gearing up to make a grand appearance at the rally, out-skate the legendary Fishballs, out-popular the celebrated June July, disseminate copies of the Manifesto of Strange to the out-of-town kids, and be crowned Rally Queen, or whatever. She MUST be stopped!

—OK, must run home now, will write more in a bit—

Later

AHHAHHAHHAHAHAHAH! I am back in the game. When I got home, I practically flew (cautiously) upstairs and (silently) rigged a lovely, lovely trapdoor right outside the bedroom. When EvilOne woke up and tried to leave the room, she fell

brrrr

through it into a chute that dropped her, screaming, all the way through the stairwells of the house into the basement, where she landed in the huge antique birdcage, where she is currently shaking the bars, mad as yarbticks, spitting and threatening me.

Am grateful for the training of Venus Fang Fang!!!!!!

On to the next stage. Will report back later.

Later

Stage Two complete. Have erased all sixty-seven copies of the Manifesto of Strange and put them back exactly as I found them.

Later

Stage Three complete. Have completely ruined November December's reputation with hundreds of teens by simply being myself. It took all the guts I had to show them my most pathetic side, but it was EXCELLENT! Clutched FakeCat to my heart, hung out with my finger up my nose, borrowed someone's skateboard and bailed out spectacularly on it, and succumbed to crying spell when I was mocked. Fishballs has won the Best New Trick competition, and all the zombified teens have adopted HIS signature look.

I finally left when half the kids there shouted at me to go. And let me tell you, it felt GREAT.

Fishballs and some of his new followers.

Later

Stage Four: Must make sure Mom is on board with my plan. Have reviewed stills from cat-cam for potentially incriminating shots. I think these ones should do it:

Later

Interesting developments! Have showed the stills to Mom. She did not need to be convinced that it was EvilOne and not me doing the deeds.

ME: See, you can tell it's her if you look at the shadow falling on her leg here, because I actually have a small chafe mark there from the cast, and . . .

MOM: Cool your jets, E, I can tell it's her.

ME: You can? How?

M: Oh, I've always been able to tell you apart.

ME: [Floored.] But how?

M: There's really no mistaking it. Facial expressions, body language, your voices, the way you smell . . .

ME: So . . . but . . . OK. Hey, so would you agree that she's pure evil, or what?

M: Well . . . . I . . . . sure. Yes. Sort of.

ME: [Punching air with fist. Hootin' and hollerin'.]

M: So what's your plan?

ME: Well, I have to let her out of the cage pretty soon. She's got to go to the skate rally so she can get pointed and laughed at.

M: Come on. That's just petty revenge, there. What we need here is a real solution.

ME: Oh. Yeah. I don't know, kill her?

M: [Not finding this funny.] Okay, I really hope you're kidding, E. First off—I thought I raised you better than that. Remember? We don't kill in this house? Also, I thought your Jeopardy game established that neither of you is really complete without the other. Wasn't that your whole point?

ME: [Blinking like a dum-dum. Proverbial lightbulb turning on in head.] Of course. My whole point. All along. Thank you. For the reminder . . . . I have to go now.

Good old Mom!!!!!!

Later

Current thoughts:

1. EvilOne and I are each just HALF of Emily Strange.
2. This helps to explain why neither one of us is all that awesome of a person.
3. EvilOne's evil HAS to be stopped, and I think the best (only?) way to do that is for our 2 halves to be rejoined.
4. I think that if I can somehow unite our bodies, our personalities will re-merge.
5. The best way I can think to do this is through drastic surgery.
6. Am resigning myself to life as a set of surgically conjoined twins.
7. As long as it means the end of crying spells and uncontrolled nose-picking. (Oh, and unmitigated evil, of course.)
8. Am looking forward to being able to lie again. All this truth-telling is really cramping my style.
9. Not sure what will become of my skateboarding skills when I have 4 legs. Am hoping for the best.
10. If all else fails, can look forward to some rewarding work in sideshows.
11. Fingers crossed that my cats will like me again once my 2 halves are united.
12. Fingers AND toes crossed that I can get EvilOne to sit still for drastic surgery.

13. Am thankful for the training of Venus Fang Fang and Queenie Kew!

Later

Stage Five complete!

I went and bought EvilOne a nice (VERY nice) new skateboard and took it down to her in the basement. We had the following pleasant sisterly chat:

ME:	Hey, Ev—OtherMe. Sorry about the cage, man. No hard feelings?
EVILONE:	I'm gonna RIP you, and TEAR you, and—
ME:	And sorry about breaking our old skateboard.
EO:	LET ME OUUUUUT!
ME:	C'mon, you're not gonna be mad about a little CAGING, are ya? After you made me think Mystery was dead? You gotta admit, you got me way better this time around. I mean, you saw all that sobbing, right? Don't ya know, I pretty much wanted to DIE if Mystery was gone.
EO:	[Calming down. Smiling a sinister little smile to herself.] I did get you pretty good, huh.
ME:	[Encouragingly.] Yeah. You did. And I know the big skate rally is this evening, and you were probably planning to go, so I got you a new

skate. Deluxe model. It's pretty king. Already put some stickers on it so no one'll know it's new.

EO: OK then, fair's fair, but you gotta let me out RIGHT NOW or I'm gonna miss the Best New Trick competition.

So I unlocked the cage and let her out.

She walked toward me with a smile on her face. A smile that, a few days ago, I might have mistaken for remorse and reconciliation. Thank you, Venus Fang Fang! I saw the violence and malevolence and, OK, a little craziness in that smile, and braced myself for what was to come.

She approached me, grinning, reaching out for the skateboard. But I saw the tiny shift in her weight as she began the vicious sweeping kick that should've knocked my legs out from under me. But as her foot lashed out, I stepped back out of range, raising the skateboard over my head.

"This one's for Mystery," I whispered to EvilMe, and administered her anesthesia. Am very glad now that I saved my pain medication instead of flushing it down the toilet. Swallowing one of those little gems really helped me get over the sting of guilt at knocking EvilMe unconscious with her new skateboard. "Sorry about the violence, Venus Fang Fang," I said, and got ready to operate.

Later

Was interrupted by urgent call from Venus Fang Fang before I was even five minutes into the operation. Things have taken a bad turn! Um, I mean, a GENUINELY BAD turn! Lots has occurred with very little time for journal writing. Am finally able to jot down what has happened. Here goes:

1. Binary Larry has taken his revenge for November December's public cruelty!

2. And has told the police that I was responsible for the Manifesto!

3. But he was laughed at, because EvilOne had already contacted the police and told them that OUR MOTHER was responsible for the Manifesto!

4. Venus Fang Fang got wind of this through her ratfink son and locked him in his room as punishment!

5. She also wasted no time alerting me that the police were coming for my mother!

6. I have hidden Mom in the secret sewer, armed with Raven and several gallons of white paint, just in case they need to cover up my highly incriminating sewer mural!

7. But pesky crying spells are preventing me from handling the situation in a calm, professional manner!

8. Now I'll have to postpone the operation until I have put the police off Mom's trail!

9. And restored the townspeople's sanity!

10. And then I'll have to deal with an enraged EvilOne, who will never allow me near her again without extreme resistance!
11. And somehow subdue her enough to surgically join our bodies!
12. And somehow make the cats like me again!
13. And concoct suitable comeuppance for Binary Larry!

July 2
Oddisee hours logged, 6; antidotes created, 1; self-confidence units restored, 2,366

I dropped some food down the chute to EvilOne. She doesn't deserve any kindness from me, but twinges of guilt were keeping me from focusing on my Manifesto problem. Clearly I am far too nice.

Then I hunkered down at the Oddisee for a serious code-fest. Now I ache all over from programming for so long, but I have (finally!!!!) succeeded in writing a Manifesto of Normal, which can be played just like a regular music CD and uses various harmonics and frequencies to strengthen all of a person's Positive Qualities (honesty, patience, kindness, sensitivity, cheerfulness in the face of adversity, what-have-you) while taking the sap out of all their Negative Qualities (lying, thievery, idle mischief, petty cruelty and violence, and so on). It should do a stellar job of neutralizing the effects of the Manifesto of Strange and transform all the raving lunatics into well-balanced, tolerant, peaceful folk who are unlikely to give me any further trouble.

I think it's a very good thing I did this before trying to surgically join myself to EvilOne, or it never would have turned out so benevolent. I really had to restrain my own idle mischief, and even so I could not help inserting a few amusing (and harmless!!!) hidden effects, such as a fondness for black licorice, impressive yo-yo skills, the compulsion to count to 13 before opening a door, the inclination to say "Flathering jimjars!" every now and again . . . you know, fun stuff.

Later

Am sitting in the reception area of the Silifordville psych ward, waiting for the supervising physician to see me so that I can deliver the Manifesto of Normal. And babbling catquacks, this place is overflowing with loonies! The receptionist looks like she has not slept in days and is constantly paging orderlies to come and restrain patients and take them away to their rooms. Every time they round up a few and cart them away, seven more wander back in here. Total chaos.

Am feeling very guilty about the mess my Manifesto of Strange caused!!!

Will try to regain a karma point or two by dedicating the next few minutes to thinking up something really nice I can do for the townspeople once they are restored to sanity.

Three minutes later

I have it! Am going to stage a one-golem circus, starring Raven! Am loving this idea. Am going to call Mom right away and let her know!!!

(Note to self: Golem Circus = FANTASTIC name for a band.)

Later

UNHOLY BEJEEPING FLAPJARKS!

They have thrown me in a room with a bunch of loonies and locked the door!

Here's how it went down:

When Dr. Greenblatt came into the waiting room, I was on the phone with Mom, having the following conversation:

Me:	Yeah, I'm gonna stage a golem circus in the park and invite the whole town.
Mom:	You're cutting out! Reception down here in the sewer is terrible.
Me:	GOLEM CIRCUS! GOLEM CIRCUS!!!!!
Random Loony:	Violet does scuttle shaky lovely very!
M:	You think that's what the townspeople want?
Me:	Yeah, Raven can, like, rip off her own arms and legs, and I can reattach them!
Dr. Greenblatt:	Yes, miss? You insisted on seeing me?

ME: Catch ya later, Patti. [To Dr. Greenblatt.] Here, I made you a Manifesto of Normal. Just play it on your PA system and it should put everyone back to . . . well, normal.

RL: I've been washing them ever since, but alas, I cannot get them clean!

DR. G: A what, now?

ME: Actually, "Manifesto of Normal" is kinda misleading, because I think you would agree, Doctor, that "normal" humanity is pretty terrible, right? So it might be more accurate to call it an auditory amplifier of all those human qualities that make up "goodness": honesty, patience, kindness, sensitivity, cheerfulness in the face of adversity, what-have-you.

DR. G: Come again?

ME: It's a Happy Ray. Just play on it your PA system, and it's gonna fix everyone up.

DR. G: Oh, how nice. You made a mix CD? And it's going to HEAL EVERYONE???!???!!

ME: [Starting to realize how loony I sound.] Yeah, I . . . uh . . . yeah.

DR. G: [Eyes narrowing.] Orderlies!! Restrain this girl and take her away.

ME: Hey! Wait! NOOOOO! Let go of me!!! I'm not

crazy!!!! [Trying to hand Dr. G the CD.] Just play the CD! Just play it!

RL: It just doesn't work out! Just leave me alone! JUST A PEPSI!!!!!

And they hauled me away, kicking and screaming, and threw me into a room crowded with drooling maniacs!! Am hiding under a bed to avoid getting any human filth on me!!!! Have GOT to break myself out of this place!!!!! But not just yet. I mean, it's a bit of a dream come true for me, being hauled away kicking and screaming, and thrown into a room full of drooling maniacs. Am going to enjoy it for a few minutes more.

Five minutes later

Gigi Doubleton, President of the Silifordville Science Club, has just crawled under the bed with me, singing "Have You Never Been Mellow" at top volume. Am done enjoying the loony bin.

Later

Man, if only Venus Fang Fang could have seen the obstacle course of loonies, orderlies, and flying human filth that I just conquered, I'd totally earn a shiny black star!!!!! See diagram for details

Crowning jewel of my escape was jimmying the grate off the air duct with a tool crafted in mere seconds from the zipper pull of Gigi's loony-bin jumpsuit and worming my way into the

heating system. Am now hanging out in said air duct just above the receptionist's desk. As soon as she steps away, I will pop out and play my Manifesto over the PA, then bust myself out of here. It's been entertaining, but I can only take captivity for so long!

Later

Sat in the air duct for ten full minutes being a total coward. Could not work up the nerve to jump out and start up the Manifesto because of crippling paranoia that I would then find myself unable to open a door without counting to 13. Would be caught by the orderlies, trapped inside the loony bin, and hideously, irreversibly Normalized. TERRIFYING!

Deliciously terrifying!

Anyway. That did not occur. The front door was open and no one saw me fleeing for my life. Am now back at home, preparing to restart the operation on EvilOne and me, and trying to get a hold of Mom to tell her it is safe to come home.

Later

Finally got through to Mom. Terrible reception in that sewer. She refuses to come home until I have proof that the Manifesto of Normal worked. Not much I can do about it right now, so I might as well move ahead with Stage Six of Operation . . . uh . . . Conjoininination!

OK, here goes—back to the surgical birdcage . . .

(Side note: It's comforting to know that, at the end of the world,

when all other conceivable combinations of letters, numbers, and hieroglyphics have been used as band names, I'll still have Surgical Birdcage in my back pocket.)

Later

More paranoia. Am sitting outside the basement door, trying to work up the courage to go back in and face EvilOne again. Am recalling my empathy training and trying to get myself into her head. I know that she's going to be infuriated AND on her guard. Sure, she has limited resources in there, but she's got all my booby-trapping skills! She could probably cobble something together out of her own fingernails and hair!!!! And she will never let me into the cage without some kind of horrendous assault. Cannot think of any foolproof way to snare her.

OK . . . I give up. Am creeping to Venus Fang Fang's house for help.

Later

Am proud to say that as soon as Venus Fang Fang opened the door, I had a flash of intuition, empathy, or whatever, and knew exactly how she would answer me . . . "McCowen-Llewelyn Maneuver?" I asked, and she nodded. Of course!!!! I slapped my forehead and made like to run home, but she stopped me. Call me psychic . . . but once again I knew what was coming.

VENUS FANG FANG:	So . . . your plan for defeating your saster . . . do you have it all set?
ME:	[Trying to lie. Failing.] Sort of.
VFF:	Does it invalve any kind of stakeout?
ME:	[Exerting superhuman effort to lie for Venus Fang Fang's sake. Succeeding, kind of.] A . . . little bit . . . of a stakeout . . .
VFF:	[Lighting up all over.] I have samthing for you.
ME:	[Graciously accepting the spy diaper from her.] Fangs. Fangs a lot.
VFF:	Have we talked about your speech impadiment?
ME:	No time for that now, I'm needed at the stakeout.

By the way: I just want to point out how tiresome it is that I'm constantly being asked by the adults in my life what my plan is, as though I'd just graduated from high school and were, like, lounging around in the pool instead of getting a job, or something. I mean, they really need to take a moment to appreciate how feggling hard I am working on resolving this whole evil doppelgänger problem, and quit bugging me!!!!!!!!!

OK, outburst over. Am feeling better. Let the booby-trapping begin!

Later

Am very pleased with myself! Not only was I able to use the McCowen-Llewelyn Maneuver successfully against EvilOne, so that she is now completely immobilized in a tight body-fitting net and suspended over a tank of deadly fish, but the net is made from spiderwebs that we/I collected, preduplication, and the deadly fish are electric eels that we/I raised ourselves. MYself. So not only is this booby trap EFFICIENT, it's also PERSONAL. Style points!

OK, am commencing operation now, let's hope it is a huge success!!!!!!!!

July 3

tar units, 23; sutures, 1 million; lame halves of self reunited, 2

EvilMe and I are one!

—Physically, anyway.

I went ahead and wore the spy diaper. Not because I planned to lose control or anything. But just as a symbol of Venus Fang Fang's support.

Cutting an incision down the length of my own body was one of the hardest things I've ever had to do. But it was nicely balanced out by the pleasure of cutting an incision down the length of EvilOne's body. Then came the stitching. LOTS of stitching. And not just flesh, but dresses, tights, and shoes as well! Do you have any idea how stiff shoe leather is?????

Then I dabbed all the sutures with liquid black rock, just to speed things along, and sat down to concentrate on joining our personalities.

But I couldn't feel her in there with me. She was certainly being shy, I thought. Or trying to hide. Didn't want to let go of being Raw Evil, maybe.

So I went in search of her a little. Called out to her with my mind. Drifted around our two joined bodies, wondering where she could be.

And eventually . . .

ME: EvilOne?

EvilOne: Oh. Is that what you call me now?

Me: There you are. C'mon, let's join forces, what do you say?

EO: I don't like you. Go away.

And she disappeared.

Um, and that's kind of where it stands right now. Have come out of deep meditative trance and left the birdcage. At least I have control of both bodies. Not that I'm not clumsy.

Am lurching around the house trying to get better at using EvilOne's side of the body and/or integrate the two of us. Would like to find her journal, which I have never even seen. Might be helpful. You never know.

Later

I fixed our cable reception and have been monitoring the news for evidence that the Manifesto of Normal is working. Did not have to monitor for long before I saw a newsflash on the "incident" at the nuthouse last night, with touching footage of a tearful Dr. Greenblatt describing the "little girl in black" who saved the town with her Happy Ray. Authorities spent most of yesterday giving loonies their shot of normalcy, and everyone has been so pleased with the results that even non-loonies are now clamoring for a dose.

Yeah. You know how, sometimes, the more Normal you try to

make things, the Stranger they become?

In other news, yo-yo and black licorice sales are up.

Later

Things are not as awesome as you might think they would be right now, considering I have two conjoined bodies. EvilOne has been weakly trying to take control of her body again. Just now she was picking at the stitches with her left hand and smacking me in the face with her right hand, which was nothing but rude. I had to stop scrounging under Mom's mattress for the journal and enact an obligatory Jekyll/Hyde-style scene, you know, where the left half of the body is battling the right half? And, to make it more difficult, I was periodically breaking off into hysterical laughing fits because it was all so very scary/stupid/comic, and then I'd feel very glad I wore the spy diaper, and that would set me off into a worse laughing fit, and pretty soon there was a line of drool hanging off my lip and I could barely get a breath.

EvilOne wasn't responding well to the laughing, but then she kind of backed off a little. That was about an hour ago. I can feel that she's still hostile, though. Will have to think up something fast. Have to return to sewer hidey-hole now to tell Mom it's safe to come home. Have been back and forth to sewer hidey-hole so many times in the past few days, I'm practically wearing a path in the street. Plus, it's not going to be easy getting to my secret entrance with no one seeing my bizarre new body. Wish I had made a secret passageway leading from my bedroom straight into the sewer. Oh well, maybe in our next house.

Later

Turns out, Mom didn't react quite as positively to my conjoined selves as I'd expected.

When she stopped screaming, I gently explained to her how I'd performed the surgery, and how I was working to get the two halves of my personality reunited, and that everything would be just fine once I accomplished that.

Mom disagreed. Loudly, with hysterical crying.

MOM: You think everything will be FINE? The police are after me! And . . . LOOK at you!

ME: But Patti, the town's back to normal! I fixed everything!

M: That's not how the criminal justice system works, E. SOMEONE will have to go down for that prank of yours!

EvilOne chose that moment to try to choke me. It took me a couple minutes to get back in control. Actually, I had to get Raven's help.

When it was over, Mom said a bad word.

Mom said more bad words, then a few more, then mixed them

up in creative linguistic combinations for new, startling effects. Then she looked at me and apologized for her potty mouth. I was just starting to say how very entertaining it was for me to hear her curse (and much better than hysterical crying) when we all heard footsteps coming from around the corner. Mystery hissed, Raven got ready to attack, Mom grabbed a paintbrush loaded with white paint, and then . . .

Binary Larry ran into view.

I yelled at Raven to grab him.

ME:	You ratfink! You told on us!
BINARY LARRY:	Aieeeeee! Freak! Monster! Gahhhhhhhhh!
ME:	Hush up or I'll tell Raven to squeeze. How could you tell on us? HOW COULD YOU?
BL:	Aihhh . . . gehhhhh . . . didn't tell on you . . .
ME:	I KNOW you did!
BL:	Nuh, I told on HER! [Pointing to my other half.]
ME:	So . . . you knew?
BL:	Yeah, I knew! And I was just GOING to your HOUSE to look for EVIDENCE!!
ME:	Well then, what are you doing down here?
BL:	[Uncomfortable silence.] Er . . .
ME:	[Sharp intake of breath.] Let me guess.

	Secret passageway from your bedroom?
BL:	Kinda . . .
ME:	I was wondering how you got out.
BL:	Er . . .
ME:	OK. Fine. You will be forgiven entirely if you can get back to my house and find the EvilOne's journal. I'm sure it's FULL of evidence. But I really doubt you'll find it.
BL:	Chaaaa, I bet your mom knows.
MOM:	What, Ev—Jem—the other Emily's journal? Yeah, she keeps it in the cereal cupboard, behind the Boo Berry.
ME:	[Stunned, embarrassed silence.]
BL:	[Stunned, embarrassed silence.] Boo Berry, huh? That box must be pretty stale by now.
ME:	[Trying to maintain dignity.] [Whispering.] Just . . . go.

And he left on sneakers of wind. Um, on legs of fire. Oh bagdarfs! He ran away really fast.

Later

Mom and I have had one of those mother-daughter chats where the mom tries her best to paint a grim picture of the daughter's future and the daughter sits in icy silence, thinking about what a dum-dum her mom is and whether boys would like her more if she changed her hair/clothes/skin/teeth/eyes/name. Except that in our case, I was actually thinking that Mom had some good points about how it could cramp my style down the road to be conjoined twins, and that I might want to think up a plan that involved separating our bodies. Have told her I will consider it.

Later

A particularly strong attack by EvilOne has made me pretty eager to consider it.

Later

Still waiting for Binary Larry. Still chatting with Mom to pass the time.

ME: Hey, Patti. I'm starting to catch some memories from EvilOne, like what "nothing but a thin broth" means. But I still don't know why we move so often.

MOM: [Dryly.] Really? You have NO IDEA?

ME: It has something to do with the dark code, doesn't it? We're on the run from the FBI, aren't we?

M: [Sighing.] If only it were that simple. What do you want, a top-13 list? You think we've never done ANYTHING to require us to leave town,

	unexpectedly, in the middle of the night, with no forwarding address?
ME:	.... K, point taken. But hey, speaking of this dark code, what is THAT, anyway?
M:	Uh . . . I think it's pretty much every code you've ever written.

Later

Binary Larry is back! Ahhahhahha! He has the journal! It is so incriminating! There is something deeply evil on every page. Here is my favorite Evil sentence so far: "June 21. I really need to find a way to surgically extract PatheticMe's guitar skills before I kill her." Furthermore, I now know what she was planning to do with those sixty-seven copies of the Manifesto of Strange: "July 1. Tonight is the big skate rally, and kids will be here from all over. I've made copies of the Manifesto and will instruct them how to set it up in their own town halls at home. Soon they ALL will answer to November December!"

Am shuddering in horror! I definitely need to separate myself from EvilOne now, so she can go down for some of the many crimes she admits to in these pages. Let me just say that she is responsible for most of the burglaries and nearly all of the vandalism that has happened since the Manifesto. And the ones she didn't personally carry out, she programmed Raven to do! She is going to do some serious time for this!

Have just caught myself with my finger up my nose again. Am recalling that I need EvilOne's qualities. Oh, and what if I DO succeed in taking all her qualities and separating my body from hers? With no personality to animate it, will her body die? And if it does, then A) can we still get her dead body to take the blame for all her crimes, and, more important, B) will I be a murderer?

Do not want to be a murderer, even to get rid of EvilOne.

Am in what you might call a little existential pickle right now.

Later

Mom has (FINALLY) agreed to leave the secret sewer and come home with me. She is nervously gripping EvilOne's journal and looking around for police officers. Raven is somehow managing to tote Mystery's cat carrier AND keep a steel grip on EvilOne, who is struggling under the Victorian tapestry we wrapped her in. And I'm holding Great-Aunt Millie's shoe box, silently conferring with her on the next stage of the plan.

Later—back at the house

Have inhaled Great-Aunt Millie! That's right, I held her up to one nostril and sniffed her right in! Now she is hanging out inside me, looking for EvilOne, so she can perform the spiritual equivalent of the surgery I did earlier today! Am patting self on back for thinking this one up!

247

Have made many preparations, and finished by filling a kiddie pool with the remaining liquid black rock. Am running so low on black rock, I had to tip out the reservoirs in the duplication device and wring out my cast. Whatever it takes! Am about to lie down in it. Am going to try for deep trance state. It's time EvilOne and I had a real heart-to-heart. Ha. Ha. Ha.

Later

Yeah, so, here's how THAT went down:

I floated there in the black rock for a while, getting into a nice meditative zoned-out state of mind, and visualized myself, my halved personality, hanging out here in this half of my body. Just hanging out, but paying attention: listening, watching, focusing my awareness on my other half.

Finally started wondering where Great-Aunt Millie could be and whether she was still here.

The answer came from miles and centuries away:

GREAT-AUNT MILLIE:	Yesssssssdearrrr I'mmmmsstillllll here.
ME:	Great, you can talk again?
GAM:	It'sssssseasierrrrr beinnnng inssssssssside.
ME:	Can you find her?
GAM:	Sheeeeeee'sssssshidinnnnng.
ME:	Any suggestions?
GAM:	Trrrrrrry gettinnnnnngbiggerrrrrrrrr.

So I visualized getting bigger. Like my self was growing to expand into every little corner of my joined bodies. Filling nooks and crannies with my spirit. And finally cornering EvilOne . . . in my left little toe.

Before I knew it, Great-Aunt Millie had zoomed up to her, thrown her over her knee, and was giving her a mighty paddling.

GAM: That'sssssssforrr thebarrrrrrrrellllll of brrrrr-rokennnnnnnglassss!

EVILONE: Aieeeeeee! OtherMe, save me!

And I did! I grabbed her away from her righteous, violent, dead great-aunt's spirit, and put my arms around her, and told her everything was gonna be all right.

ME: We belong together, EvilOne!

EVILONE: You just want your skateboarding skills back!

ME: No, no, it's not like that, I swear . . . I mean, you're ME! And I'm YOU! And you might be evil in its rawest form, but gobbing loquats, I NEED YOU!!!!

EO: Do you realize what we're doing?

ME: Um . . . hugging? And learning?

EO: That's right.

ME: But there's something else going on here, EvilOne. You see, the whole time I've been

hugging you with my SPIRITUAL arms, I've also been using my PHYSICAL arms to tear out the stitches that were holding our bodies together, and now it's time for us to be TRULY ONE AGAIN!

EO: Noooooooooooo!!!!!!!!!!

And as the essence of EvilOne flowed from her body into mine, I ripped our bodies apart bit by bit, holding her spirit tightly all the while. Oh the pain pain pain, but there was no time to think of that. I was getting stronger and more powerful, more MYSELF, and the other body was being drained of life, black stuff, Strangeness, Evil, skateboarding skills, and whatever else was animating it, until it looked all pale and limp, like an old corn husk or dried-up snakeskin.

I was about to snip the last few stitches and separate us forever when Great-Aunt Millie spoke up.

GREAT-AUNT MILLIE: Waaaait jussssssssssta minnnnnnute, mydeeeeeeeear.

ME: Yeah?

GAM: Sheeeeee stilllll hazzzzzzzz yooooour lazinesssssss, deeeeeeceit, annnnd pettyyyythieeeeeverrrrry. Shalllllllll

weeeleeave themmmmm wiiiith
herrrrrrr?

ME: Nah, I need that stuff.

GAM: Whatabout nozzzzzepickinnnng an
cryyyyying spellllllllls?

ME: [Suffering the old existential pickle.] Uhhhhh . . .
I better keep everything, just to be safe.

Shellac! Am hoping I made the right decision. I considered being choosy about which qualities I took back, I really did, but remembered what Mom said about no killing in the house. I actually take that seriously, you know. And if EvilOne had ANY of my human qualities left, it WOULD be killing. I really didn't want Mom or Venus Fang Fang to think I murdered EvilOne.

Later

Excellent! Mom agrees with me that what's left of EvilOne is no more than a VERY large, unusually detailed, eerily lifelike hangnail sort of thing, and can be cut off with no guilt whatsoever!

Used the toenail clippers to snip her away from me. And let me tell you, it felt GRRRRRRRRREAT!

Later

Back in my bedroom. MY! Not OUR. Had a very emotional reunion with my cats. I did not cry. I DID NOT CRY! HAHAHHAHHAHHAHHAHAH!

July 4
moms still paranoid about police, l; senseis enlisted to help
save the day, l

Woke up at nightfall when Mom knocked on my door. She is still
fussing over the possibility that the police are coming after her.

Not knowing what else to say, I suggested we talk to Venus Fang Fang about it tomorrow. After all, it was HER son who put the police on our trail . . . maybe she'll feel obligated to help out.

Gotta go, I have a wicked new park to skate!!!

Later

Have skated the very pudding out of every rail and ramp. Local teens made way for me, with odd looks aplenty. I guess I should be embarrassed, considering the last time they saw me, I was weeping/clutching a stuffed animal/picking my nose . . . but it just felt so good to be skating, and I really couldn't care less about anything else.

Here's the weird part, though: Skating that park was all new to me, AND at the same time it was all completely familiar.

Later

Back at home! Good times! Have spent most of the night play-ing guitar at top volume, revamping all the basement booby traps, and (most important) petting cats. It is sooooo good to be myself again. Will never mess about with self-duplication again!

Later

OHHHHHHHHHHHHHH NOOOOOOOOOOOOOO!!!!!!

It's three in the morning and I just got off the phone with Binary Larry. Here's what he had to say:

BINARY LARRY:	Dude, I didn't see you in the sewers tonight.
ME:	Nah, my mural's all done, and I got other stuff going on . . .
BL:	Yeah, well, as long as you got some pictures, I guess . . . I just thought you'd want to, like, give it a farewell touch-up or something.
ME:	What do you mean, farewell? I'm not going anywhere.
BL:	Well, you KNOW, that whole thing? With the mayor?
ME:	WHAT THING???? SPILL IT RIGHT NOW, YOU!!!!!
BL:	Dude! Don't you watch the news? They're gonna flood our secret sewer with poop!

Yes. Yes. Earlier tonight, apparently, the mayor announced that it was high time the town revisited the original purpose of the ill-fated ribbon-cutting ceremony, which I never bothered to discover. Oh flabbering gutbarks! It was supposed to be the inauguration of the brand-new sewer system! They are indeed going to flood my lovely, lovely sewer mural with filth!

I realize there is really nothing to be done about it but am going to sleep on it and see if I come up with some kind of plan. Sad end to a great night.

July 5
incredible nightmares, 1; grand Ravenesque fiascos, 0 (I hope???)

Wow.

Have just had THEEE MOST AMAAAAZING nightmare!

Poor Silifordville! Poor poor poor poor Silifordville!

—Uh, I think the town is actually OK, but this dream was just so flathering REAL—

OK. Here's what my very own golem did in my nightmare:

- Ripped free all the walls of the new sewer system. (Not just north- and east- facing walls, either.)
- Punched them up through the pavement, destroying pretty much all of Silifordville's roadways in the process.
- Slammed the muralized walls down onto the cars of Silifordville, flattening them all.

The creepy part was how the townspeople reacted. Since everyone was Happy Ray'd into ultimate benevolence, no one tried to stop her; they just stood by patiently and watched her do it. Then the mayor publicly thanked "the little girl in black" for giving the town of Silifordville such beautiful new sidewalks, eliminating the cars that were polluting the air, and providing a reason for the town to switch to composting toilets. Then she dynamited the dam and let Lake Siliford flow into what used to be the sewer, creating a lovely canal system in place of the roads.

AHAHHAHHHAHAHAHAHHAHHAHHA!!!

Man, I LOOOOOOOVE a good nightmare.

Later

Was feeling so invigorated by my excellent dream that I actually didn't feel quite so awful about the defiling of my mural, and left the house ready to take on the night. Skated down to the sewer for one last look at my masterpiece. Had to laugh at my ridiculous dream. If I HAD asked Raven to save my mural, she'd be much more likely to do it by scraping the paint off the walls and gathering the flakes up in her pockets, or something.

Packed up my paintbrushes, leftover snack treats, candles, surveyor's gear, mapmaking gear, and spelunking gear. Took some final farewell photos and hightailed it out of there just as the floodgates creaked open and the avalanche of yukness poured in and ruined my mural forever. It's OK, though. I think I

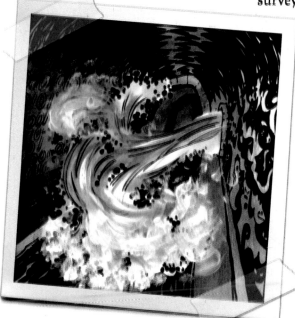

prefer knowing it is down there under the muck, rather than on the surface, being used as a sidewalk by the Silifordvillians.

Later

Came home from the sewers late for my appointment with Mom and Venus Fang Fang. The two of them were already deep in discussion.

ME: So lay it on me, Venus Fang Fang. Do you
                           think you can help us convince the police
                           that Patti didn't do . . . ahem . . . that
                           awful, evil prank down at Town Hall?

VENUS FANG FANG: Oh, that would be no prablem at all. You
                           see, I knaw who ACTUALLY did it.

ME: [Wide-eyed, innocent stare.]

MOM: [Mortified silence.]

VFF: I also knaw why you left Blandindulle,
                           Dullton, Dumchester, Ridicaville, and
                           Tootleston.

ME: [Sarcastically.] Gulp.

VFF: [Glaring at me.] I've also discovered eight
                           hidden effects of your Happy Ray. And if
                           I know your habits at all, which I do, I'll
                           soon find anather five.

ME: . . . . [Gulping for
                           real now.]

VFF: I ALSO know about a fairly long list of incidents invalving your dark code. Not to mention, I have some pretty good ideas on the significance of that liquad black rock of yours.

ME: .... Oh. Um. OK.

M: [Carefully.] What do you intend to do with this information, Mrs. Fang Fang?

VFF: I'm advising, and I hope you'll decide to consider this advice <u>VERY CAREFALLY</u>, that you leave Silifordville pratty much immediately.

ME: But . . . I thought my training was going so well . . .

VFF: I haven't made many mistakes in my career, but I made a very sarious one by training you. Had I known that you and your so-called saster were two sides of the same person, I'd have been much more cautious.

ME: But—? What—? Why—?

VFF: Don't you wander why I trained YOU, and not HER?

ME: A lattle. Ahem. A little.

VFF: I would never offer my skills to anyone as deeply evil as your . . . ather side.

ME: But how do YOU know she was evil?

VFF: I tald you she became good friends with my dog, Viscer . . . well, I followed them on their

258

walks and saw how she used that friendship.

ME: Oh no, let me guess . . .

VFF: It's all raght. I intervened before anyone was actually mauled. But now that your two halves have reintegrated . . .

ME: Venus Fang Fang, you don't actually think I'M evil . . . . . . do you?

VFF: No, no. I'd say you're HALF evil.

M: [Indignantly.] Mrs. Fang Fang! My daughter is NOT half evil!

ME: Uh . . . Patti . . . ?

M: 49% evil, I'll grant you that.

VFF: Please don't be offended, Ms. Strange. I myself am roughly half evil. Young Larry . . . prabably 52%. Can't train HIM. Sweet chald, though. But Emily here happens to have . . . unusual talents, very dangerous in the hands of even the half evil, definitely warning signs of future Evil Overlordish tendencies. Just 13 years old, and she's already implicated in several unsolved cases of industrial sabotage, defacing of public sculptures, and in a couple of instances, the mostly complete destruction of small towns with funny names.

ME: Well, then, wouldn't it be better if I stayed here, where you could keep an eye on me?

VFF: Oh dear, no. I would have no problem keeping

an eye on you no matter where you went. But I'm not the only one watching, and we don't want to attract the wrong kind of attention. It would be a grave tactical error for us to stay in the same town together. Not just for your sake, but for mine and young Larry's. And, well, we were here farst.

M: No problem, Mrs. Fang Fang. We're, uh, pretty used to this.

VFF: Splandid. And I will settle everything with the police.

Me: [Getting mad.] Wait, so I have to pack up and move all my stuff AGAIN, just so I don't inconvenience YOU? This is all about your super secret sewer, isn't it?

VFF: My . . . super . . . secret . . . sewar.

Me: Yeah, what, you didn't think I knew about that? What do you have hidden down there, anyway, that's so fribbling important?

VFF: [Long, thoughtful pause.] All raght . . . I owe you that much. Come by my house tomarrow evening and you'll find out.

Gahhhhhhhhhhh! Am of course extremely curious to see what she's got in there, but it's small consolation for having to move again.

July 6

lethal nerve gas units, 0; ancient relics, 0; pots of money, 0; copies of <u>Defeating Your Enema</u>, 0; Mr. Fang Fangs, 0; spy labs, 0; spy diapers, 0; china units, 0; refugees, 0; monsters, 0; summoning chambers, 0; apocalypse supplies, 0; command centers, 0; martini glasses with silly straws in them, 6

Raven and I are hanging out in the super secret sewer, which contains Binary Larry's swanky, futuristic BACHELOR PAD! AHHAHhahha-hAHHAHHHA!

I let him believe he was entertaining me.

BINARY LARRY: The great thing about binary is how versatile it is. I mean, two people who knew it really well could hold hands and use two different finger squeezes to have a totally secret conversation!

ME: Yeah, sounds great, except it would take hours to say anything interesting.

BL: [Looking dreamy-eyed.] I know!

ME: [Snorting.]

BL: Did I ever tell you about my friend Hex Lex, who carves messages in hexadecimal in the sidewalks with a hammer and chisel?

Later

Raven and I have paid a final social call on the ladies of the Silifordville Science Club. Bebe is still her same old self, having refused a dose of Happy Ray, but Gigi is a changed woman! I can't say I like her new style much, but she's much less argumentative than before, and she overflowed with positivity when I showed her the dried-up husk of my former evil twin. I encouraged her to keep it as a rare scientific specimen. And also to gross out Bebe.

Later

Back in my bedroom with the Posse. THIS IS THE LIFE. Lounging on the bed, putting off packing, writing in my journal, getting pawed at and headbutted by Sabbath, blanketed by Miles and NeeChee, gazed upon with love (and some drool) by Mystery . . .

Mom has just knocked on my door complaining that SUDDENLY no cats want to sleep with her anymore. I offered her my well-worn plushy FakeCat. She tried to turn it down, but took it in the end.

July 7

procrastination units, 3; boxes packed, 1,749; new towns chosen, 1

We are practically done packing already! Oh the joys of a well-programmed golem! I'm about to tape up my last box of critical personal items, and it's time to pack away this diary and get on the road. One last to-do list before I wrap this up:

1. Must get duplication device working again. With way more safeguards this time!!!!
2. Mom clearly needs a vacation from me. Must see about sending her on a long cruise to foreign places.
3. Lots of band names, zero bandmates. Must train cats to play instruments.
4. School will be starting all too soon. What excuse will get me out of going this year?
5. Should begin brainstorming next Master Prank ASAP.
6. Might want to sniff out any lurking spy trainers before starting next Master Prank.

7. Should stake out territory for my next mural. Bigger square footage. Less potential for being defiled with sewage.

8. Is the world ready for an English-to-Catlish translator, and do I want to give it to them?

9. Having successfully made golems out of Tasmanian devils, possums, ravens, discarded glue bottles, and staple guns, I think it's high time I tried creating life from scratch.

10. Am out of liquid black rock. Must arrange return trip to ancestral home soon to refill!!!

11. Not sure whether to be more offended that Venus Fang Fang thinks I have Evil Overlordish tendencies OR that she doesn't seem to consider this much of a threat.

12. Should really investigate what Venus Fang Fang actually knows about me and how she got her information!!!

13. Venus Fang Fang = KILLER name for a band!!!!!!!!!!!!!!!!!!!!!!!!!!!!!!!

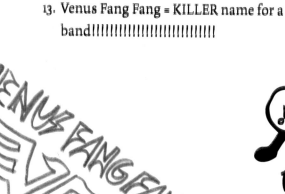

Still strange after all this time!
Watch out for

Emily®
the Strange
Dark Times

13 intriguing aspects of Emily's next diary:
1. The glorious Time-Out Machine
2. White fever
3. Dark elixir
4. The return of Attikol
5. Great-Great-Great-Great-Great-Great-Great-Great-Aunt Lily
6. Spiderweb embroidery
7. The 1790s
8. Forbidden fruit
9. Gritts, cyder, and molasses
10. Bloodletting
11. Severed cat tail
12. Parallel universes
13. Dark girls